PRAISE FOR A

C000200579

Small Fo

"A spellbinding, intoxicating journey into the dark heart of obsession.
... another beautiful, heart-wrenching, epic masterpiece. I loved it."
Tom Gillespie, author of The Strange Book of Jacob Boyce

"A soulful tale of painting, secrets and longing, which draws the
reader into a world of mystery and memory - an enchanting read."
Leonora Meriel, author of The Unity Game

"It's beguiling, haunting, beautifully paced and it kept me hooked
to the very end."
Michael Walters, author of The Complex

Grace & Serenity

"The gripping story of a girl´s downward spiral to the bottom. A
FINALIST and highly recommended!"
The Wishing Shelf Book Awards

"The story of a desperate young woman who finds herself on a
difficult path, and hurtles towards a thrilling conclusion. A tense and
compelling read."
- Vikki Patis, author of In the Dark

You. I. Us.

"It's expert storytelling and skilful writing when so much is expressed
in so few words..."
- Cathy Ryan, Between the Lines

"These honest stories are deeper and more expansive than the words
on the page."
- Ann S. Epstein, author of The Great Stork Derby

THE CLOCK IN MY MOTHER'S HOUSE

and other stories

ALSO BY ANNALISA CRAWFORD

Cat & The Dreamer

That Sadie Thing and other stories

Our Beautiful Child

You. I. Us.

Grace & Serenity

Small Forgotten Moments

THE CLOCK IN MY MOTHER'S HOUSE

and other stories

Annalisa Crawford

For Mum
for the laughter
and for the inspiration

CONTENTS

THE CLOCK IN MY MOTHER'S HOUSE RUNS BACKWARDS

"I can't believe you kept it."

It's a hideous thing—a Year 8 woodwork project that should have gone straight into the bin. Scarcely circular, infuriatingly oval in fact, where I'd over-planed it to make continual yet ultimately fruitless corrections. The hour increment marks are unequal as the chisel deviated around the grain. The brief called for a pendulum which I designed in the shape of a cat dangling by its back legs, with flecks of orange emulsion for eyes. This eerie, withered creature watches us.

"Oh, it's a cat… I always wondered." Mum sets two mugs on the coffee table and stands beside me with her head tilted to match the accidental angle of the stupid cat.

"Well, I think it's a cat. It still doesn't work."

Only after I brought it home did we realise the mechanism was going backwards. Dad attempted to fix it, spreading the cogs out on the dining table and running his fingers through his beard. I took it back to my DT teacher who tinkered with it one lunch time. Neither of them could resolve the problem, and I thought we'd thrown it away.

"I found it in the loft. I like it."

"Where's your stick?"

"Oh, it's… somewhere." She waves her hand dismissively, casting a cursory glance around the room. "I forget to use it sometimes."

That's a new one on me. Usually she's reliant on it, shuffling along tentatively, or catching her foot on the carpet and using it to right herself. Today she's straighter, sprightlier. She moves without her habitual groans.

Later, as I kiss her goodbye, I glance at the clock. Yep, still ugly.

We meet up once a week, usually at Mum's house. She struggles to get out much; she feels more secure at home. She likes routine; she likes to use the same mug, the right brand of tea.

The next time I see her, she seems taller. I sidle up beside her to measure myself against her, trying to judge the comparative heights of our shadows on the wall. She was always a couple of inches above me—an adolescent bugbear that my growth spurt stopped short of her five foot seven. The dark, puffy shadows beneath her eyes are smoother and they've lost their opacity.

"Have you lost weight?"

"A couple of pounds." Hands on hips, she shimmies to show off her rediscovered waist. "Oh. Look at the time!"

I glance at my ugly cat clock. "How can you even tell the time on that thing?" I watch the hands turning for a moment, captivated by the absurdity of it.

Mum fusses with her bag and dashes into the hall for her jacket. I trail after her. She checks herself in the mirror, fluffing her fringe, pursing her lips.

"Are you wearing make-up?"

"Yes, I've got a date," she says reticently.

"A date?"

After Dad died a couple of years ago, Mum showed no interest in meeting new people, content to sit in front of the TV or pottering in the garden. The suggestion of joining a club was ignored.

"Who with?"

"Someone from Bingo. You don't know him."

Between visits, Mum phones, though we never have enough to say to warrant it. Once the pleasantries are done and she's enquired after Kevin and the boys, we fall into a laboured stream of random topics —the weather, the state of the roads, which neighbour has gone on holiday. She likes to hear a familiar voice, she says, rousing my guilt. Without me, she says, she'd be lost.

It's been three days since I last saw her, and yet no call. I phone, but she doesn't pick up. An hour later, I try again and let it ring for longer. After several attempts, I start to worry. I leave work early, citing an emergency, and rush across town to check on her. I imagine her lying on the floor in pain, unable to call for help. I shouldn't have waited so long.

"Are you okay?" I ask, when she opens the door to my panicky knocking. I scan her face for bruises and her limbs for plaster casts. "You haven't called."

"Of course I'm okay. I've been busy, that's all."

I lean against the door frame to catch my breath. "Busy? But I've been worried."

"Whatever for?" She laughs. "Come in. You'll have to excuse the mess. I'm having a sort out."

Piles of clothes are strewn across the sofa. Ornaments she's had for years have been cleared from shelves and boxed haphazardly. I gaze with concern at these once-beloved items—presents from Dad, from long-deceased relatives, a framed painting I gave her for her birthday last year. She bends to scoop items off the floor. Bends!

"You love this dress." I hold up a dusky pink shift she wears for

13

Christenings and weddings, and scan the boxes for the matching hat. It has a faint odour of mothballs.

She swipes the dress from my hand and drops it into a bag-for-life. "It's frumpy."

"You've dyed your hair?"

Streaks of grey remain at the temples, but her brunette lustre and bounce has returned. She pats it self-consciously and smiles.

"It started turning brown a couple of days ago. Must be my new shampoo." She twirls. My broken, arthritic mother dances on the spot. "What do you think?"

"Mum, what's going on?"

"Have you eaten? We could go for a late lunch. Frank took me to a lovely coffee shop the other day—we could go there."

"Frank?"

"My friend. I told you about him," she says lightly.

She busies herself with gathering her coat and finding her shoes. I watch in confusion. Her skin is smooth, and her cheeks are plump. Her jawline is sharper.

I glance at the clock on the wall, at the hands ticking backwards, at time reversing. The monotony holds my attention, slowly hypnotising me. I forget what I'm going to say next.

I begin to visit every couple of days, curious to see if other changes occur—after work mostly, then increasingly instead of it, daily.

"Oh, for God's sake," says Kevin. "What's the problem anyway? She's doing exactly what you've been asking her to do for years—going out, making friends."

"But it's not just that, it's…" I waver. It's all so ridiculous. I ought to take him with me—he'll never believe it without seeing her in person.

Each day, Mum's increasing vitality is apparent. She abandons the elasticated waists and orthopaedic shoes for fitted skirts and vibrant colours, for strappy dresses and baseball boots.

The softness of her body melts; the prominent veins striating her legs recede.

She enjoys a brief spell of crocheting when her fingers suddenly become more dexterous but dismisses it within a couple of days for something less boring.

"I might join the gym."

She bounces away from that idea and onto something else. Heavy metal gigs, learning to surf, skydiving.

"*Deep-sea* diving," she gasps, grabbing my arm excitedly. Fresh-faced, we could be mistaken for sisters.

"Mum, stop this."

Her Lady's Friends are replaced with Cosmo, casually left open at articles about sex toys and experimenting with lesbianism. She closes the pages slowly, checking I've noticed, as if to get a rise.

Her daily tipple of sherry becomes an afternoon of Prosecco. She pours generously, and we sit in the living room, awkwardly. I censor everything I want to say—starting and restarting conversations in my head, but not having the conviction to carry them through. The clock mocks me with its anomalous existence. I can't help but stare. The creepy cat is daring me to intercede. I shudder under its sinister gaze.

"Dad got so mad with that clock," I say. "Do you remember?"

She's lounging on the sofa, her legs stretched over the arms, the wine glass resting on her flat stomach. She's lithe and flexible again; her limbs long and languid.

"He tried hanging it upside down, didn't he? Stupid man."

"Mum!

She's never said anything unkind about Dad before, not even in jest. She sips from her glass and flutters her feet in the air.

"Could you imagine his surprise if he walked in now and saw you looking like this? He wouldn't believe his eyes." I try to make it light-hearted, but the air fizzles with all the things I haven't said.

Mum's legs stop swinging. Her arms are rigid across her chest.

I chew on my nail. "You know, I think we should get rid of that clock—it's obviously never going to work. I'll buy you a new one for Christmas."

Mum sits up, puckering her lips into a tight O. "No, I like it. How could I not—you made it?" She stands and edges towards the wall.

We scrutinise each other warily, each trying to ascertain what the other is thinking—like one of those old westerns when they zoom in on Clint Eastwood's narrowing eyes and play ominous music.

"Do you...?" I pause and consider. "Do you think the clock is affecting you... in some way?"

"Of course it's not. Don't be so ridiculous. What? What would it be doing?"

I gaze incredulously at my mother who looks exactly as she did on her wedding day, her skin dewy and fresh, the hint of freckles across her nose. "This! It's doing *this*." My exasperated arms swirl around in front of her. "Just... let me take the clock."

I stand and she hurdles across the room to get between me and it. "Don't touch it!"

On my way to the wall, I pause mid-stride. I don't remember the last time she moved that fast.

"It's *my* clock."

"I *like* it."

I make sharp, abrupt twitches, testing her reaction. Each gesture is mirrored, every action met with caution and unease. We're in stalemate.

"I think you should go."

My eyes flicker to the clock, relentless and unnatural. I calculate the speed I'd need to achieve to out-pace her; I note the coffee table that might impede me, the stool which might trip me. My legs are poised to leap, my arms ready to propel me.

Mum eyes me with the steeliness of a lioness.

I surrender with reluctance and let my arms relax, forcing a smile. "But I've only just got here. Do you want me to put the kettle on?"

"No, I don't think so," she says coolly.

16

She stands at the window as I walk to my car, as though I'll race back to catch her unawares.

Mum starts to look like every photo of herself as a twenty-year-old. She pierces her ears again and fills her wardrobe with skinny jeans and tight t-shirts. I'm certain I spot the red raw swelling of a new tattoo peeking from beneath the hems.

I tidy up when I go over—scraping burnt baked beans from her pans and throwing out a pile of empty microwave meal trays. I pour rancid milk down the drain and gag at the mould on the bread.

Every time I leave, I fear what I'll see next. I make ludicrous plans to steal the clock, to break in when she's not at home. I wake in the night, or don't sleep at all.

"It's not possible," I tell myself.

"It's really not possible," I say out loud to Kevin, who grunts and rolls over.

On Saturday, after sending Kevin and the boys to the cricket, Iron Maiden blares out as I turn into her street, and it takes a moment to realise it's not coming from one of the other houses, but from *hers*.

"Oh, for crying out loud," I mutter to myself and hold my finger on the doorbell so it resembles an infuriated wasp. I've got a key, but I'm scared to use it, worried what I'll find inside.

A neighbour slows down as she passes, switching on her gossip antenna, making notes for the next WI meeting. I smile tightly and say, "Lovely morning." She quickens her pace and disappears around the corner.

As I consider retrieving my key ring from the bottom of my bag, the door opens. My eyes are level with where Mum's should be, but she barely reaches my shoulders now. She's almost a kid again. She steps back silently and lets me into the house.

"You can't take the clock." She scrunches up her freckled nose and scowls with defiance.

"Really? You want to go all the way back to being a baby, do you? You want me to carry you around in a sling?"

She hesitates, plucking a retort from mid-air. "It might not be the clock at all. I've had it in the house all this time—it might be something else entirely."

"Like what?"

And her argument falters. I reach to take the clock off the hook. She jumps at me, trying to obstruct me or knock it from my hand. She pulls on my arm, but I shrug her off easily. She lets out a long, high-pitched screech and pushes me repeatedly.

"Stop that!" I scold, and she stumbles backwards.

I hold the clock above my head, and she stares with horror.

Tears roll down her chubby cheeks; her bottom lip quivers. "Please don't."

I yank the mechanism from the back, rip the hands off, throw the battery across the room. I stomp down on the plywood until it cracks; I grind my heel and it splinters.

The silence sighs, shrieks, squeezes.

It holds us, suspended.

We're captivated, breathless.

Mum's limbs begin to stretch. Her torso lengthens. Bones crack and tear. Her hair grows.

Her nose loses its buttonness; her freckles fade.

Acne covers her forehead and cheeks fleetingly, then vanishes. She reaches my shoulders, then draws level—gangly and awkward, then immediately spongy and plump.

Her hair grows, thick and shiny.

She's taller than me again. Her breasts protruding, and her waist shapely and defined.

For a second, she hits the sweet spot of clear skin, juicy lips, bright eyes, contentment in her own skin.

Wrinkles appear, laughter lines form in the corners of her eyes and mouth. Her jawline softens, jowls form.

Her hair grows, hanging limply, flecked with grey.

Dark spots spread across the back of her hand and décolletage; blue veins swell beneath her skin. Hips billow.

Her hair reaches her waist, a straggly wave of silver.

More wrinkles. Deep creases, like valleys, criss-cross her cheeks.

Her fingers curl and refuse to straighten. She holds them out to me in distress and flinching with the pain of it. Eyelids droop. Hips creak.

Her skin is paper thin; knuckles large and inflamed. Her hips are generous and her dress strains around them.

Her eyes are hollow, withdrawing into their sockets. Lips brittle; her face gaunt. Her skin is loose as though I could pull it away from her skull.

A lifetime's ageing in sixty seconds. Older now than I've ever seen her. Too old.

Shrinking, folding in on herself. Shorter than me, reaching out to me with skeletal fingers.

She stares in terror because it doesn't stop.

THE WOMAN IN THE VAN

She appeared overnight. On the breeze, people will say when the story folds into folklore. Because that's how small towns flourish, isn't it, on stories? Whispers spread from friend to friend, neighbour to neighbour, through the generations.

It was a warm evening, by all accounts, when the painted caravan rolled into town, pulled by a beaten-up Morris Minor which barely had the strength to do so. It stopped in the large overflow car park reserved for height-of-season holidaymakers. Empty now. Tourists recalled to everyday lives, kids returned to school, the town drifting into its autumnal lull.

People diverted their routes to walk past the van, the following day, glancing inquisitively as they headed to the tiny train station for their tedious commute. A steady stream of traffic wound down from the high road, across the valley, and up the other side.

Not until mid-morning did she throw open the door at the back of the van to sit on the wooden step—inhaling the fresh air flowing from the coast and soaking up the weakening sun with a smile of contentment. She took an apple from the pocket of her long, brocade skirt and cut it with a paring knife, eating slices directly from the blade.

When the apple was half-eaten, she set it down on the wooden floor of the van and watched a uniformed shape stride across the car park towards her. The old woman hobbled to the edge of the lake a few feet away and bent to dip her hand into the freezing water.

"Hello, love," the shape called as she approached, "beautiful day, isn't it?"

The woman remained where she was, staring down at her fingers fluttering in the water. "Aye. It'll turn soon enough, though."

"What's your name?"

The woman turned, shielding her eyes from the sun as she peered up. "Hester."

"I'm Kate. This is an interesting van."

The badge on her jacket said Police Community Support Officer, and Hester hmphed to herself. "It's legal." She returned to the step, took the apple, and resumed her dissection.

Kate smiled amiably. "I'm sure it is." She reached to inspect one of the rust patches on the car, pushing against the metal to scrutinise the integrity of the chassis.

Hester focused on her apple. She crunched into another slice and wiped away the juice as it trickled down her chin.

"The thing is, you can't stay here," said Kate.

"It's a car park. I have a car."

"Yes, but it's not an overnight one. We don't allow trav... people to camp here."

"I won't be in the way. I'm early, that's all. I'm here for the boy."

"What boy?"

Hester broke into a slow, half-toothed smile and shook her head. "Ah, don't mind me, just the ramblings of an old woman."

"Where have you come from? Is there someone I can call?"

"Do I look like I can't look after myself?"

Kate pursed her lips. "No, but—"

"Well then…"

"But you can't stay here. There are no amenities. Perhaps you'd be more comfortable at the campsite. It's about a mile away. It has electricity, and bathroom facilities." Sensing the standoff which was occurring, Kate reached for her radio.

"I won't cause trouble. I keep myself to myself."

Kate sighed and lowered her hand. She glanced towards the main street, then back to Hester. This wasn't the result she'd hoped for. The neighbourhood sergeant wouldn't be happy. She manoeuvred to peer inside the van, to generate a valid reason to move her on.

The walls were deep burgundy, with a row of cupboards on each side, and a bed at the end. Pots and laundry hung from hooks in the ceiling, and a clutch of dreamcatchers dangled from a curtain pole. Tarot cards and a crystal ball were shoved into a corner. Messy, dirty even, but not hazardous.

"I used to tell fortunes at fairs," Hester said.

"Oh?"

"Would you like me to read your palm? I do that too."

"Oh, no thank you."

"I'm sure you'd be fascinating to read."

Kate shook her head. "I have to get on. A couple of days, you said, then you'll be off?"

"Aye."

The PCSO nodded her reluctant consent and said goodbye.

***

Leon hid from his dad. He hid from his teachers and friends. From the police. From the neighbour whose greenhouse he'd smashed with a miskicked football.

He hid from the bullies, too—the ones who blocked his path and jeered at him, who demanded money and punched him so hard he thought he might have to hit back. Even though his mum would've disapproved. She'd taught him there was always a better way. So, he hid away and waited for them to get bored.

That morning, the same morning Hester opened the doors of her van, he was stripping out of his school uniform behind the shed at the bottom of the garden.

"Time for school," his dad called from the back door. "Leon?"

If he waited long enough, his dad would think he'd already left. He'd rinse the breakfast dishes and make his way downstairs to the gift shop he owned.

Leon's dad was trying his best. His mum's death had been sudden and unforeseen. The gulf she left gaped between them during every meal, each awkward encounter in the kitchen and half-committed conversation. Leon needed a hug, but there was no one to provide it.

He listened and lit one of the cigarettes he'd nicked the day before.

"Loser. No one smokes anymore," said the girls in his Maths class, and Leon thought 'no one' pretty much summed him up. He took a couple of drags and stamped it into the mud.

It was just gone nine when Leon opened the back gate and, after glancing at the rose bush his mum had tended so carefully, left. On summer evenings, once they'd eaten tea at the plastic camping table and his dad was reclining with a beer, his mum would fuss with the weeds growing around it or prune its browning leaves with secateurs. It was dying now, the rose. Neither he nor his dad had green fingers.

Leon sauntered down the back lane and out onto the street, with trepidation. Skipping school seemed an easy option, but the hours between nine and three-thirty were interminable. He had to dodge friends of his mum who'd smile with pity, then tell his dad he was right to let Leon take time off, inadvertently giving away his skiving. He couldn't wander around the shops or sit on the beach—everyone knew him.

He kicked a can which rattled along the pavement, accelerating as it hit the camber. He took the back streets, crossed the main road, and strolled through the car park towards the public footpath into the woods. Hands shoved into his pockets, shoulders hunched to conceal himself, he stared at his feet scuffing the tarmac.

Even Leon, hiding in his own world, couldn't miss the bizarre caravan painted with wild colours and swirling patterns. He turned his head so he could study it as he walked past. An old woman sat in the open door stared back just as interested in him.

A few paces later, he vanished into the trees. His destination was ten minutes along the narrow mud groove which served as a path. He veered left and climbed a small embankment, using tree trunks to propel himself up. And there it was, just as they'd left it all those months ago.

His mum discovered it, originally, on one of her afternoon walks. A small, derelict bird hide. She went back several days in a row, to ensure no one was using it, then took Leon with her. He was nine at the time, a quiet thoughtful lad—she thought he'd like it. It became their special place. After school and during the holidays, they'd pack snacks and head out. Leon's dad was invited but always declined.

Leon glanced behind him, in case the last few months had been a terrible mistake and his mum was following. He longed to hold out his hand and help her up the final few steps. Wind bristled through the trees, a bird cried out, two grey squirrels danced along the branch just above his head before zipping away.

Leon tucked himself into the slatted wood frame and pulled the tarpaulin down. It was dark now, save for a shard of daylight shining through the slit in the fabric for birdwatchers to peer out.

They'd never really cared about the birds, although one year he'd bought his mum a guide to British birds for Christmas, which they'd used for a while. Mostly, they huddled together with a flask of hot chocolate and shared secrets.

It was weird being there without her. Alone, it was just a decrepit wooden box. The floor was unyielding, and the air was dank. His mum talked with such exuberance he'd never noticed the discomfort.

She told mesmerising tales of her life before he was born—confiding the sad parts, the lonely parts, the desperate parts. Her eyes shone when she reached the day she met his dad, the day they got married, discovered they were going to have a baby. He always hoped there'd be time for the story of his birth, which was in a middle of a thunderstorm, when the power lines went down, and the midwife couldn't be reached. He was born by candlelight; his dad delivered him.

Leon didn't stay. He'd planned to hang out there all day—his bag stuffed with snacks—but it was wrong now. He watched the shabby tarpaulin flapping in the wind. A bird sang from high up. He tilted his head, but the branches were too dense to make it out. He swung his bag onto his shoulder and shuffled down to the path without looking back.

That caravan was still there, and the woman still perched on her step like a little bird. He skulked past, so not to attract her attention.

"Shouldn't you be in school?"

"Shouldn't you mind your own bloody business?"

The woman smirked. "You're probably right. I'm too old to care, anyway."

"Uh." He kicked a stone. "What're you doing here?"

"Just passing through."

He eyed her guardedly. She looked the way his mum might have, in years to come, dressed in an array of colourful layers, and patched-up jumpers with ragged sleeves dangling over her hands—unlike any old lady he knew.

She stood with a grimace, pushing one hand against her hip to straighten herself. "Would you like some tea? I've just made it."

He shrugged. It was too early to go home; someone would see him. Someone would give the game away. "Whatever."

The steps creaked and the caravan rocked as she moved inside, muttering to herself. She returned with two mugs, both cracked and stained. The tea was dark. Leon took a sip and baulked at the tannin.

"Ta," he said.

"Do you have a name?"

"Leon."

She nodded with satisfaction. "The lion! It suits you." She took a sip. "I'm Hester."

The conversation stalled. Leon drank the overbearing tea one tiny mouthful at a time.

"I've got biscuits inside."

"Nah, I better go."

"Mum waiting for you?"

His eyes watered, and he fought them away with a snarl. "She's dead."

It came out harsher than he intended. How could he say it in such a hostile way? Usually, his voice softened when he talked about his mother—although he couldn't remember the last time he'd actually said her name aloud.

"Ah. I'm sorry. She must have been a wonderful woman."

He drew himself up, defensively. "How would you know?"

"I know her son, and he's a fine young man."

"You don't know me."

"I know you stayed and drank awful tea with a doddery old lady. Not many fourteen-year-olds would do that."

"I'm sixteen."

She watched him thoughtfully. "So, it's an important year for you, at school? Exams?"

Leon scuffed his shoe against the tarmac. "I guess."

He glared, challenging her to say more. But she didn't. She drew her sleeves up her arms, bearing her skin to the warming sun.

"Are those tattoos?" he asked, pointing to the green fading lines snaking towards Hester's elbows.

She pulled the sleeves back down. "Yes."

"Cool. How many?"

"I lost count. They help me to remember people."

"Cool." The initial interest waned. He looked around, breaking the bond. "I'd better get back. See ya." He paused mid-turn. "Thanks for the drink."

Leon stood in the kitchen with his coat still on, and contemplated cooking something for tea. The flat above the shop was a frosty shell without his mum. Nowhere felt comfortable or relaxed.

There were eggs on the side, chips in the freezer. He prodded the small bag of salad in the fridge, brown and slimy, and wondered what his mum would have said. She always loaded their plates with fresh fruits and vegetables from her patch in the garden. She'd never have allowed a bag of salad in the house.

They weren't, Leon determined, particularly good at looking after themselves. They were pathetic without her.

In the living room, he gazed at the photos on the wall. Right after she died, they vanished—hidden somewhere Leon couldn't locate. One by one, they were reappearing, as his dad felt strong enough to see them again.

Most of the pictures were of Leon himself—on fairground rides, on benches with one or other parent, digging trenches into the sand, crouching beside the neighbour's dog. As an only child, he was doted on. Everything he did was captured by video or photograph. He'd watched his first step and his first words so many times.

His mum smiled out from several pictures. He reached to touch her cheek, pretending she was beside him. The front door slammed shut, and he jumped away from the wall.

***

The next day, early, Hester walked to the shops. She could see the top end of the high street from her van, but her faltering steps, and pauses to cough and wheeze and lean on her stick for support, made it a much longer journey than it ought to have been. People stared as she passed them. The butcher's fell silent when she walked in, and people turned away as she joined the queue.

She ambled the long, narrow street of surfing and gift shops until she reached a road on the left which snaked past a terrace of stone cottages and up the hill.

Gripped with fear, her breath stolen for a moment, Hester leant against one of the houses. She saw the boy, Leon, swathed with an impenetrable grey fog. He was reaching out for her, but before she could reach him the vision faded.

It was nothing she hadn't already seen, of course; it was the very same premonition which had brought her here. But in situ, it was more terrifying and intense.

"You all right?" The real Leon materialised in front of her, startling her.

"Oh, hello. Yes, just a little unsteady. I wanted to see the sea, but I don't recall this being such a long street." She held out her arm. "Would you walk me back to my van?"

"The sea's not far, if you wanted to carry on." Leon nodded along the road to where the terrace abruptly stopped and shoved his hands into his pockets.

"No, I think I've done enough for today."

He didn't take her arm, but he took her shopping bag and walked alongside her. He kept a metre distance between them, so although they were together, it didn't appear that way.

"Tell me, what's up there?" Hester gestured back to the junction.

"Just the cliffs. The road goes to the top of town and turns into the coast path. Ain't much to see except the view, I guess."

"Have you always lived here?"

"Yeah."

"I was born here. I was seventeen when I left." Hester paused; the strain of walking and talking catching in her throat. "This is the first time I've been back." She glanced at Leon who stared at the pavement with indifference. "I was born in this house right here."

They'd reached Leon's house, and both looked up at the narrow three-storey building.

"It wasn't a shop back then. We lived in the top rooms, and two other families lived below us."

"That's my house."

"Oh," said Hester. "Is it?" And she shuffled onwards.

"Are you a witch?"

Hester chuckled. "No."

"But you can see the future?"

"What makes you say that?"

"Heard people talking in the shop." He avoided her eye, blushing intensely.

"Yes, people do talk, don't they?"

They plodded on, towards the bridge which united the two sides of town. Every so often, Hester rested to catch her breath and Leon waited discomfited beside her.

"Can you tell me my future?" said Leon in one of these pauses.

She was caught off-guard. "Why would you want me to do that?"

"Coz…" He hunched forward as if trying to make himself small and insignificant.

"You're thinking of your mum?"

"I'm always thinking about her," he replied, his voice snagging.

"I know. It must feel so hopeless right now, but it gets easier."

"How do you know?"

"Because I'm an old woman. I've lost people. And I've seen other people lose people."

"Then tell me my future, tell me when."

She sighed. "I don't read for children. Your future isn't fixed. It's like an ocean, flowing in all directions, nothing's settled until you're much older."

They were at the edge of the car park now. Hester thanked him for his help and for the conversation, and he ran back the way they'd come.

*

There was no electricity in Hester's caravan, so night-time settled upon her much quicker than everyone else. She had an oil lamp but rationed its use to spare the fuel. At seven-thirty, she tucked herself into the compact bed and listened to the sea wind gusting around, buffeting the van as though it had no weight at all.

As her eyes closed, she thought of Leon, and the misery he was suffering. Then she drifted to the others, to those immortalised on her skin, the people she needed to remember—those she'd saved, those she hadn't. An audible sigh of regret escaped her lips.

Creeping fog blunted the noise of the town settling down for the evening. Hester peered through the curtains and saw nothing at all; even the streetlights had vanished. Her heart pounded in her chest until she could scarcely hear anything else. She fidgeted with one of her beaded necklaces. It was time.

***

After Leon's dad closed up the shop, he went out for takeaway, and stomped back upstairs to the flat. They ate in silence, straight from the polystyrene box, in front of the TV showing something neither of them was watching.

"Where were you today?" asked Leon's dad, tightly.

"School."

"No, you weren't." He put his fish and chip remains on the floor and opened a can of beer. He bent forward, resting his elbows on his thighs. "Your teacher phoned. You haven't been all week."

"It's only Wednesday," Leon muttered.

His father's hand slammed onto the arm of the sofa. "That's not the point!" He took a breath and glanced at the photos on the wall. "This is an important year. You want to do well, don't you?"

"Don't need to. I'll work in the shop with you, no biggie." Leon shrugged and pulled batter off his fish.

"That's giving up, taking the easy way out. You want to stay here forever? There's so much out there just waiting for you, so much for you to experience." He sighed. "What would Mum say, eh? You think she'd want you to ruin your chances of a good life?"

"It doesn't matter what she'd want coz she's not here. Nothing matters anymore."

"You're being ridiculous."

"Me?" Leon pushed his takeaway box off his lap and it fell to the floor. Chips scattered.

His dad's temper was escalating again. His face was reddening. Leon wanted it that way; he needed those emotions to surface and endorse everything he was feeling himself. He'd been trying so hard to bite back his own anger, but it was too big—there was too much to carry around.

"School's not optional, you know. You don't get infinite excuses."

"Yeah, well, I guess if I didn't love her so much I could just carry on, like you."

Slap! Leon's face throbbed. His dad recoiled, staring at his hand as though it was alien to him.

"Leon, I—"

Leon stared at the TV, tears prickling his eyes. He focused on the melancholy faces of soap characters who were discussing the death of another. He reached for the remote and switched it off before he could absorb too much of their distress.

"I'm sorry. I didn't mean—"

Tears slid down Leon's cheeks. "You never spent any time with her, you were always working in your bloody shop. She told me. She said that."

Slap!

Leon gasped. "I loved her so much," he yelled. "Why didn't you die instead? It should have been you!"

And he ran. Not just from the room, but from the flat. Bolting out the back door, through the garden, and into the side street. He ran until he was sure his dad wasn't following. He ran until his lungs were ready to explode and his legs were jelly.

He replayed the fight. Imagined himself saying even worse things, unforgivable things. The slap became a punch. Several punches. In his head, he hit back, and his dad went sprawling across the floor.

Fog swirled. Not the usual sea mist, but viscous and saturating. The shadows of buildings loomed over him. His agitation had scrambled his sense of direction. He wasn't certain where he was.

He wanted his mum. She wouldn't have let him do stupid shit like this.

The town was foreign tonight. Landmarks chopping and changing, relocating to confuse him. The fog swarmed as though it was alive, as though he could reach out and hold it. Leon leant on a lamppost and wrapped his arms around himself.

Gradually, the anxiety dissipated. He settled into the silence and the chill vapour on his skin became a delicate touch, his mother's affectionate hand on his cheek, as though she was beside him, where she ought to be.

He wondered how high the fog went, if he could stand above it. He was walking before he had chance to consider, gradually regaining his bearings. The next junction would lead to the steep coast path the old woman asked about. He braced himself for the climb.

Eventually, at the top, he caught his breath and turned to look. The town was blanketed, obliterated. Pinpricks of light emerged from the gloom, before being obscured again as fog crawled through the valley. Leon took a step forward. The ground crumbled beneath his foot, and he lost his balance.

In her caravan, Hester stretched blankets taut around herself and squeezed her eyes shut.

She waited, her heart heavy with apprehension.

She stared into the mottled blackness.

*

32

It was midnight when the alarm was raised, when Leon's dad realised his son's absence had advanced beyond its permissible duration. He gazed from the window and could barely make out the road below. He checked Leon's room a second time, but the bed was still empty; the room had the crispness of disuse.

A search party quickly assembled—a coastal town is always ready. The lifeboat was put on standby; neighbours and friends gathered in the square. Groups were created, and sections of the town allocated among them. It happened in a flash, it seemed to Leon's dad—one moment he was in front of the TV, the next standing in a scarcely visible street describing the clothes Leon had been wearing and the fight they'd had. Personal information. Not for public consumption.

These people knew their troubles, of course. They'd attended the funeral, and brought them stews and lasagnes and homemade pasties to save him the bother of cooking when their grief was raw. People had bought him a pint when he sat forlornly in the pub. A couple of them had even volunteered in the shop while he was too distraught to work.

He looked into their eyes, standing in the fog, and was ashamed he needed their help again.

The search parties peeled away, heading to the areas they'd been assigned, towards the outskirts of town, the beach, the woods. They muttered words of support or patted Leon's dad on the shoulder as they left.

"He goes to the woods a lot," said Leon's dad, though by then it was more of an aside as few people were left to hear him. "Used to," he added, feebly.

Leon's name filled the night, the only sound perceptible above the solid air. Leon's dad added his voice for a while, then fell silent to pray. He didn't pray, normally. Even when his wife was suddenly struck down and on life support, he held her and urged her to fight, but he didn't pray, he didn't beg a divine presence to intervene. But Leon was all he had left.

*

Torches were ineffective to light the path, acting merely to indicate the location of the bearer, flitting like fireflies. Hester monitored their progression through her window and dressed to greet them. A helicopter circled for a few minutes, then moved towards the sea, slow and resolute. The search beam highlighted the swirling damp air.

"You're looking for the boy?" she asked, when the dark shapes revealed themselves.

"Yes. Have you seen him?"

"He's not here. He's on the cliffs, above the beach." She closed her eyes and held her fingers to her temples. "He's hurt. He fell."

"We're searching everywhere. A group will be at the beach soon. We're heading into the woods."

"But he's not there!" she cried out in despair.

One of the stragglers patted her arm. "We know what we're doing, we'll bring him home safely. Go inside and get yourself warm." And he dashed away to catch the others.

"No, no…" Her voice went unheard. She paced back and forth. She was supposed to prevent the tragedy, not witness it. If she let events play out the way she'd seen, if nothing changed, what was the point of her being here?

Leon's frozen hand curled around the thick root and he tucked himself close to the cliff. His feet tried to gain purchase, but the shale crumbled away as his weight pressed down. The root creaked and loosened; the damp fog made it slimy beneath his fingers.

He tightened his grip, trying to ignore the black drop and the waves splintering against the rocks below. His fingers slithered along the root, and he cried out.

Hester grabbed her oil lamp from the van and lurched across the car park. The light shone against the fog rather than through it, making it seem like a wall, concealing the space beyond.

She shuffled, allowing her free hand to trail against the railings and shop fronts. The lamp was heavy and unwieldy.

The helicopter was aimless now, filling the sky with the relentless swish of its blades.

"Leon… Leon…" The refrain was harrowing, catching on the air without reply.

Hester stumbled on a kerb and took a moment to steady herself. Her eighty-two years were onerous when she needed to be spritely; they were an anchor, a hindrance.

"Stupid old woman," she muttered, tapping her stick ahead of her, checking for uneven paving slabs. The last thing anyone needed was to have to rescue her as well.

But she couldn't give up now; she'd come all this way to save the boy, and she needed to carry out that task. She closed her eyes and took a breath, aligning herself with the layout of the town, before setting off again.

The voices grew fainter as the search broadened.

"Leon… Leon?"

"Hello?"

"Leon?"

"No."

Two figures appeared in front of her, and she clutched their arms with an emaciated grip.

"Oh, thank goodness. I know where he is, the boy—he's up on the cliff."

"It's okay, love. Did you see him go that way?"

"No, but I know he's there. You have to go to the cliff."

The two men glanced at each other, with dubious frowns. "No, love," said the older, "he wouldn't be up there. That road's not safe in the dark. He knows that. He's a sensible lad."

"But he is. I dreamt it." She shook her head, brushing her words aside. "I *know* it. You have to save him, before he's hurt." Her voice splintered, and her legs quivered. "Please. You have to."

35

The other man, his son perhaps, a fledgling version of the elder, reached out to stop her collapsing. "No one goes up there at this time of the night. Why not go back to your van and wait for news there?"

They were growing impatient, shifting their feet to move past her.

Hester held herself tall. "Very well, if you don't, I will."

She pushed between them and walked determinedly.

"Wait."

She disregarded them with a flourish of her hand, and mulishly continued her path as the gradient took an unexpected severity and she was forced to slow down. The men caught up in seconds.

"Okay, okay. We'll go. You stay here." And they scurried up the road, sucked into the fog.

Hester pulled her heavy greatcoat around her gaunt body, and slowly trekked after them.

Knees, ankles, back, they all ached. With every step, she wondered if it was too late. Her lungs filled with damp air; her cough rattled. She leant on her stick, unable to go any further. She listened keenly; the silence more evocative than before.

Leon's arms fatigued. His fingers cramped. His feet were sliding off the small ledge.

He tried to call out, but the words stuck in his throat.

He imagined his mother beside him, holding him up.

Voices echoed through the fog suddenly, tumbling over each other. Shouted instructions were relayed. Footsteps thundered past Hester, heading for the cliff. The helicopter settled into a low hover, almost on top of her.

People oozed from their houses, standing in the middle of the road in dressing gowns and slippers. They glanced at Hester with disdain; and she returned their stares with similar. What had they been doing all evening anyway, sitting inside, oblivious?

*

A hand grabbed Leon just as his body was preparing to succumb.

The future altered.

The images in Hester's mind collapsed like a tumbling tower of blocks.

Hester's relief immobilised her. Some of the rescuers were returning, laughing with palpable relief. A couple nodded in her direction.

Only when the helicopter flew overhead, taking Leon to hospital, did her strength recover. She held her lamp out in front of her and headed into the fog, one teetering step at a time.

No one remembers when the old woman left town, so they say.

Legend has it she and her caravan vanished that night.

But equally, she could have remained for days or weeks, dining with Leon and his grateful father, drinking in the local pub with the older townsfolk.

That's what happens with stories; no one really remembers the truth.

VERA SAYS...

We call her Vera, and she takes us where we want to go. Or, perhaps, where she thinks we need to go—like the Tardis whisking the Doctor around the universe.

Vera says: Prepare to turn right in two hundred yards.

She says: At the roundabout, take the third exit.

And we obey, because she's in charge. We type in postcodes and allow her to dictate our every move from then on. When we stop for lunch, veering from her chosen route to find somewhere nice, she throws a bit of a tantrum, to be honest, instructing us to take a U-turn at the first opportunity.

Vera says: Take the first left, then the first right.

I peer out of the window. The town is behind us, fields and rolling hills ahead. Breaks in the hedgerows reveal clumps of houses and sheep munching grass.

"I'm not sure she knows where she's going."

"Of course she does," Robbie says. "There'll be a traffic jam or something—she's taking us a back way, that's all."

He scowls at the road; he's not thrilled about this wedding. His tie is digging into his neck, and he tugs at his collar. In front of us, a car is breaking sharply every time it meets a slight deviation in the road. Robbie taps the steering wheel in frustration.

"Mmm." I check Vera's screen—thirty-six minutes until we arrive. There's no signal on my mobile so I can't text to let them know. I bounce it against my thigh. "We're going to be late."

"I told you we should have started out earlier. We should make it in time for the reception."

"She's my oldest friend, I wanted to be there for the whole thing."

Vera says: Take the next left and follow the road for five miles.

"Five? Where the hell is she taking us, Outer Mongolia?"

"You sound like your mother when you say things like that." At the crossroad, he leans forward to check for traffic.

"Piss off."

I watch the white lines down the centre of the road disappearing beneath us. The gentle grind of the tyres on the tarmac is annoyingly soothing.

I reach for my bag on the back seat.

"What are you doing now?"

"Getting the invitation—it's got a map. I want to see if I recognise any place names."

"Well, can you sit still? I'm trying to concentrate."

"On what? It's a straight road."

The directions are printed on the back of a picture of the hotel. The Wilder Hotel and Golf Club is an expansive white building, fronted with bay windows and a columned porch. The grounds are immaculate, with a fountain in the centre of a majestic drive. We're travelling through freshly manured fields, nothing elegant enough to be a golf course. The hedges are unkempt; the road is peppered with potholes that send us rocking side to side. Occasionally, we slow to a thirty mile an hour limit as we wind through stone-built hamlets. Robbie speeds abruptly once the restrictions are lifted; the polyester of my dress causing me to slide in my seat.

I'm silent. Sullen and annoyed. I seek out road signs, clues. The sun vanishes behind thick, leaden clouds. "It was supposed to be sunny."

Vera says: Turn right and take the next left.

We happen across the edge of a village. Houses with lights on to combat the rolling gloom, expensive cars parked outside. It's large enough for a church and a general store and a pub.

"Why don't we stop and ask someone?" I stare at the directions in my hand. None of the place names are familiar; we haven't passed near any of them.

"We don't need to ask."

"Get a satnav, you said. We'll never get lost again. You said."

Robbie stares at me. "Finished?"

I shrug.

Vera says: Take the next right.

Our conversation pares down into soft grunts which say everything from I'm Sorry to I'm Hungry to I'm Worried.

"I'm scared," I whisper as the road becomes a bumpy lane. The trees pack tightly together, towering up and forming a canopy which curls down on top of us like clawing fingers.

Vera says: Turn right.

We peer into the leaf-shrouded shadows, drawing level with the spot Vera's indicating.

"Is that it?" Robbie points to a small indentation in the hedge where countless cars have pressed against it to make room for on-coming traffic.

"Of course it isn't. The Wilder Hotel entrance won't look like that." I hold the picture of the venue close to his face; he pushes it away with irritation.

He drops his hands from the wheel and leans back, surveying the road ahead, glancing back over his shoulder.

The wind picks up, sighing through the trees like several voices merging together.

"Okay," he says cautiously. "I'll nip in here to turn around. We'll go back to that village. We'll ask for directions." He bows his head in acquiescence.

The car squeezes through the hedge. Splintered twigs scratch the sides; waxy ivy sucks us in, embraces us. The only light comes from the dashboard and Vera's screen, our faces glowing ominously red. The foliage thickens, interlocking its branches and leaves like long-lost lovers. It tangles around us, holding us fast. Robbie revs the engine. Glass cracks.

Vera says: You have reached your destination.

ALL THE MAGPIES COME OUT TO PLAY

The woman in the house opposite sits in her window with the net curtains falling in an arch around her. She stares into the deserted road as if watching TV and waiting for the next programme to begin. At intervals, she wanders off, returning with a sandwich or a cup and saucer, and drinks with her little finger daintily extended. When she's fed up with the empty street, she reads a book.

Two magpies sit on my wall. One for sorrow, two for joy… The lyrics bounce around in my head. I used to know the whole rhyme, all the way up to ten. Three for a girl, four for a boy, five for silver, six for gold, seven for… seven for…

The woman in the house opposite is watching the birds too, and waves when she catches my eye. I wonder if she's been waving for a long time, eager for my reaction. Or if she's waving to the people next door to me and I've intercepted it. Are the people next door also looking out of their window? Are we all?

I'm not at my window, I'm sitting on the sofa against the back wall, watching Netflix—seeking out films I've seen countless times before. My mind is wandering too much to try something new, something I'd have to focus on. I drift and dream, and when I return the story isn't where I left it.

It's possible she sits at her window every day, while I'm new to this—new to the concept of being home on a weekday morning.

I wave back, and the skittish magpies fly away.

The woman waves again the next day, a brief acknowledgement as if she's unsure it's the right thing to do. Window waving etiquette is uncharted—an intrusion into someone's life, or a courteous gesture of camaraderie?

The next day, she does it with a cheery smile, and her husband stands with a hand on her shoulder. It's the first time I've seen him, and I'm glad she's got company. She covers his hand with her own and leans into him. They're looking at the small garden in front of their house—he's pointing, she's nodding.

I've never paid much attention to her or, indeed, to any of my neighbours. It's always early when I leave for work—I'm at my desk with a takeaway latte by eight—and I'm too exhausted to even raise my head on my return. I simply watch my feet trudge the pavement. My office is in darkness and silence now. Emails were hastily sent after last weeks' announcement—stay home, wait for details. Now we're adrift from normality. I ought to check my email again. Maybe later.

By lunchtime, the sun has moved, so instead of having a clear view into my house, the street is reflected back at my neighbour and all she can see is her own house, and possibly herself. I stand at my fridge, disappointed with the food inside it, longing for the enticing panini menu of the sandwich shop near work.

The afternoons are eternal and tedious. I flick TV channels and send messages to friends and read a chapter or two and clean the kitchen and vacuum upstairs and down. And dust. The same as I did two days ago—there's only so much mess a woman living alone can create.

I share memes and upload photos and comment and like. I work on a report that probably won't get submitted. I drink too much coffee and feel jittery and a little bit sick.

I've sorted through my clothes and made a charity shop pile. There are more clothes on that pile than in my wardrobe now. I stare at the blouses and smart skirts on hangers and wonder when I might be wearing them again.

Eight days. It's been eight days, silly woman.

I scan my food cupboard again. I really want some chocolate, but I don't have any. Is chocolate essential? That's all we're allowed out for—essential items. Milk, bread, cheese are essential, of course—you could live off that for weeks. Maybe add in a can of tuna or two, and some frozen veg, and you'd be set until this whole thing passes over.

I really want chocolate.

Joggers pass my house with alarming frequency—so many of them! Singular serious runners, or adults and a child, or adults with a child on a bike, or adults on a bike while a child runs beside them. Most of them are red-faced and puffing. We're allowed to exercise for an hour a day and it seems people are taking this as mandatory.

Not me, not yet. I've got a battered pair of trainers from a mud run I did a couple of years ago—the dirt still clumped to the soles. Too knackered to clean them at the time. Run, ha! More like a slog and slurp through sticky swamps of clay. I collapsed on the sofa when I got home and didn't move for the rest of the weekend. I even considered, late on the Sunday evening, taking a sickie the following day because I was sure my legs would be completely seized.

A few doors along from the house opposite, the elderly man who lives there has visitors. Three of them stand at his window and shout through the small gap he's opened. Two adults and a sullen teen on his mobile, until the woman takes it from him. She holds it as she gestures her conversation, brandishing it in front of him. His eyes fix on it like a cat stalking a red laser beam.

Outside looks nice. The sun's shining, warming me through the glass. Clouds dab the sky, like a kid's paintbrush has splatted them onto a page. Fresh air floods into the room when I open the window, instead of the usual car fumes. On a whim, I pull on my trainers and stand at the door.

The roads are emptier than the pavements. As people meet, they curve around each other, stepping off the pavement, keeping their distance. I do the same, calculating my two-metre span, turning my head slightly away from them while still attempting to smile and say thank you.

It's a strange concept, this unnatural aversion. Previously, I've only avoided people when I've been wary of them—when I've been walking home at night and not wanted to overtake the solitary man in front or the group of boisterous teens with half-drunk bottles of lager. Now, two metres doesn't seem enough. When the next person walks towards me, I cross to the other side of the road.

Despite my trainers, I'm not actually running. I briefly consider it, but my legs never increase to the required speed. A brisk walk is still exercise, though, for now.

It's cooler than I assumed. As I turn corners, wind rustles through the trees while new buds cling on tightly. Birds sing with fervour. The low hum of traffic, which usually serves as a relentless backdrop, has vanished. Between footsteps, there's silence.

Magpies sit on bowing branches, high up, sleek and shiny, blue-tinged. The same ones I saw the other day, perhaps, following me as though they've nothing better to do. No, I remember, it's not them who've got nothing on, it's me.

"Morning," says a voice from the other side of the street, and I glance up. "Lovely day."

"Yes, I suppose so."

"Weird times."

"Yes."

"At least the sun's out."

"Yes, lovely. Enjoy your walk," I say, and move away quickly lest he start explaining how he's not walking for fun but to buy groceries for a neighbour because we've all got to do our bit. Maybe I should have checked if the couple opposite needed anything. I'm sure they must by now—milk, bread, chocolate.

The shop has a queue outside, stretching almost the length of the road, with neat awkward spaces between each person. All eyes stare forward; silent panic and fear scratched into their faces. I grab my facemask—my favourite one with large orange and yellow flowers —and join the line, waiting patiently.

Someone mutters and grumbles. Another replies, agreeing it's all just nonsense, isn't it? The rest keep their heads down or play on their phones.

Magpies land on the front wall of a house along the road, three this time—they've found a friend. Three for a girl. I don't know anyone who's pregnant, so it's wasted. I want to point them out to someone, to share the happy news, but the queue moves two metres forward as the next in line enters the shop.

I'm still unsure about the necessity of chocolate. Perhaps I should buy milk while I'm here, or bread. Do I need them? I didn't look. I didn't plan to be here. I'm in trainers and leggings—I planned to go for a run. I'll tell Mum it was a run, when I phone to check on her and Dad. Everyone's doing it, I'll say.

On my way home, I place a small box of Milk Tray on the step of the house opposite, and knock on the door, then stand back until I'm almost in the road, allowing her space.

"Oh. How lovely." She frowns her curiosity.

"I wanted some chocolate. So, I thought you might like some too." Saying it out loud, my inspired idea seems a bit daft—buying chocolate for someone I've never even spoken to?

"Well, thank you. I'm Mary," she says, stepping back as though to invite me inside, then remembering.

"Jess."

"I don't think I've seen you around here before?"

"I work long hours, usually. I moved in a couple of years ago."

She smiles dolefully. "I confess, I don't know many of the neighbours anymore. There was a time, oh, long before you were born…" She shakes her head self-consciously. "You probably don't care about things like that."

"My grandmother says the same thing." I pause. "I'll be shopping again in a couple of days if you need anything. Just tape the list to your front door and I'll grab it when I go."

I'm glued to the TV for information, analysing every word, every intonation. It reminds me of photos from the war when families gathered around the radio to hear the latest news. I glance left and right and imagine others with me.

Is this it? The way the world ends? All of us stuck within the walls of our own household prison. I hear the kids next door, raucous in their freedom from school rules and discipline, and their harried dad yelling that he's trying to work. The walls are too thin—I've never noticed before. I'm hardly here, so why would I? Out early, back late, meeting friends for drinks or cinema or dinner; home is simply where I sleep.

On Thursday evening, I hear rainfall, but it's not—it's the ripple of tentative applause. I stand at my door and join in. And afterwards, people hang around. No one wants to go straight back indoors. All along the road, people are conversing and laughing and introducing themselves. The woman opposite is standing at her window. She waves, her eyes downcast. I cross the road.

"My husband's not well," she says, leaning forward and steaming up the glass.

"Oh. Is it…?"

"He's coughing, got a temperature. He doesn't want me to phone the doctor, he says he's fine and it's nothing to worry about."

"He might be right." (I gave them chocolate—did she wipe the plastic wrapper, did I inadvertently give them the virus too?)

She turns her head slightly. "Can you hear that?" Her mouth is tight as she frowns and contemplates the harsh, unremitting cough from another room. Her eyes are dull and fearful.

From the little I know of them via my small observations through the net curtains, they're devoted—they kiss each other on the cheek when they leave the room, they hold hands just because. When one talks, the other looks up with a gentle smile and listens.

"Perhaps you should phone anyway, to put your mind at ease." I want to rest a consoling hand on her shoulder, but I can't. I can't invite her to mine for a coffee and a reassuring chat either.

The doctor visits. I watch from my sofa, on the back wall of my front room. I try not to appear as though I'm looking. When she opens the door, Mary doesn't wave at me—she's pale and nervous. I phone my parents.

Days pass. I try to get out every morning, walking one day, jogging the next. Already my breathing recovers more quickly, my muscles aren't as tight when I stretch out at the end. If I'd known it was this easy, I'd have done it ages ago. Ha, no I wouldn't. Long office days and exercise don't mix well.

I attempt to read the books I've hoarded for years, meaning to get around to. But I can't concentrate—the words don't make sense. I read the same sentence four times and still don't comprehend. I've become a person who throws books across the room in frustration.

The doctor visits Mary's husband again, and she's smiling when she sees him to the door. She waves him off, then waves at me. I phone my parents.

*

In the spaces between us, birds flit on the pavement and the middle of roads undisturbed. Squirrels scamper from tree to wall, clinging precariously to scaffolding, climbing electricity poles. Weeds grow in the gaps in the kerbstones, and bees feast on the yellow and purple flowers which are flourishing. Stillness lies across town and becomes normal.

With a single turn down a different road, the air can be filled with an opera of birdsong—a camouflaged flock of blackbirds and song thrushes calling into the late afternoon. And as I run—not jogging or walking now but feeling the force of the wind in my face and the power of my legs pushing against the tarmac—my thoughts are discarded, and my mind is clear.

Days pass.

The rooftops glow pink as the sun sets. A cat slides along the red brick houses and curls around lamp posts. We stand at our front doors and clap. Someone in the next street over has brought out a pot to bang, and we tut and shake our heads. But I reckon the woman at 62 will do the same next week, and then we'll all start. Afterwards we swap recipes for flourless cakes and talk about R numbers as if we understand what it means.

One by one, my neighbours return to their homes, their doors close with reassuring thuds. Two magpies land on my fence, watching me. I salute them and go inside.

A THOUSAND PIECES OF YOU

The mirror smashed onto the floor, right in front of you. Do you remember? Concentrate. Think. It tumbled from the wall when the cord snapped and unravelled with a loud whirr. It coiled, onto the polished boards like a sluggish snake. Your heart is hammering; you're gulping for air because the oxygen has been sucked right out of you.

And your feet hurt. You dig your bare toes into the shards of glass, flinching as they lacerate your skin. Small granules grind your soles. You push your weight into the floor, and the pain intensifies.

Look at the wall. Look at the floor. Concentrate. Let the images weave together. Think. Remember.

The frame lies face down. Tentatively, you lift it and prop it against the sofa. Larger pieces of glass are clinging on, cracked and jagged. The reflections glitch. A hundred faces watch with dark, curious eyes. A thousand flashes of who you were, a million echoes of what has gone before.

You push one of the fragments to line it up with its neighbour. It slices your finger.

"Shit!"

But you don't pull away.

You press firmly, enduring the puncture it creates, twisting with reckless curiosity.

Some of the faces egg you on, urging the gash wider and deeper. Some lower their gaze awkwardly, a little embarrassed by your display of wilfulness. Others contort as though feeling the pain themselves; or perhaps feeling it instead of you. Yes, that's more like it, isn't it? Someone else's finger; someone else's suffering.

A bubble of dark blood bulges from the wound, expanding and dribbling across your knuckles. It tastes of metal when you press your tongue against the cut to stem the flow.

For a second, after the smash and the crash, everything is calm.

The front door slams. "I'm home." Max's footsteps plod along the hall. They pause—jacket removed, bag dropped to the floor—and resume.

You stand and spin around, forgetting the glass crunching underfoot, grimacing as it bites. Max surveys the chaos. His eyes narrow; his mouth an O shape, his words missing. Still sucking your finger, you're silent too. He glances at the floor.

"What did you do?"

Accusations fall easily from him these days. Your head fills with a tirade about how he should stop nagging and leave you alone, how things sometimes just happen and it's not always your fault. But the act of vocalising is too much effort. You're exhausted thinking about it.

"It fell."

You gesture the wall, to the grimy outline where the mirror was. There are scarlet gashes on your palm, little bruises forming.

"You cut yourself."

"Just a scratch."

"Your feet…"

They're still tangled among the debris, stinging when you look down—the sight of blood reminding you of the agony. Sunlight bounces off the glass, making it look like smooth white sand on a picture-perfect beach. You tilt forward to see the reflections—the versions of yourself that aren't quite you. Strangers in a crowd.

"I'm sorry," he says, a moment too late. "I just wondered if…" His hands rise and fall, a clumsy halt to his sentence.

Wicked smiles play on their lips; each moves a fraction slower than the last. You wink coyly and the duplicates emulate you. You incline your head, left, then right, and they follow. You hold a finger to your lips. Ssshh.

"Kels?"

Heads up, then down, poke out your tongues, make silly faces, Vogue like Madonna. Moving to a soundless melody, teasing, trying to catch one another out. Max bobs about too, vying for attention, but he's fading from the room, blending into the walls and furniture.

"Kelly!"

In the mirror, you're the student beside her boyfriend's hospital bed after a late-night hit-and-run. Endeavouring to understand what the doctors are saying, trying to be grown-up yet longing for her parents to arrive and take control. He'll die before sunrise. She has no idea how devastating her grief will be. You reach out to wipe mascara from her cheek.

The replicas mutate, blurring their edges until they meld together, until some aren't you at all. Spellbound, you're drawn into this mirror-land, this multitude of identities.

You're the teen who nicked lipstick to impress her mates, the girl who dispassionately denied being anywhere near the shop even after her mother found the black Dior tube and interrogated her relentlessly. You witness the insolence and swagger as she smirks at you, daring you to tell the truth.

"Kelly! Stop this!"

You're aware of Max again, though his voice is faint and indistinct like someone falling from a cliff. Like someone trapped in a giant bubble. Someone on the opposite side of train tracks trying to attract your attention above the uproar of the engines.

You're the nervous wreck at her first job interview, anxious and out of her depth. She didn't expect a panel. She's saying the wrong things; her skirt's too tight and rides up when she crosses her legs. She's intimidated; she wants to flee. She won't get the position. She'll spend her twenties jumping jobs, never quite fitting.

Max holds your elbow and guides you from the glass wreckage. You sit on the varnished wooden floor, legs stretched out, leaning forward to keep the mirror in view, twisting to monitor those fractured imposters.

You're the college graduate at Glastonbury, wild and free. Bare-chested, shirt tied around her waist; long turquoise hair adorned with flowers. Later, sitting on her boyfriend's shoulders, torso decorated with luminous body paint, she'll sing loudly to "End of a Century".

Max fetches the rudimentary first aid kit from under the kitchen sink—an ice-cream tub overflowing with out-of-date ointments and plasters which are no longer sticky. He casts items aside and holds a bandage indecisively. He leaves and returns with a bowl of water and a flannel. The smell of antiseptic fills the air, and you brace yourself for the sting.

He eases the wet flannel over your skin, brushing away the larger fragments and rinsing small slivers. Cautious and meticulous, he pulls gently on the pieces wedged more deeply, pausing when you flinch.

Each toe is slashed; some of the cuts are inflamed with flaps of skin curling away from the wound. Both feet are embedded with minute glittering flecks. The pain is dissipating. Someone else's feet; someone else's pain.

You're the euphoric daredevil in a jumpsuit, perched at the door of the plane, waving with an infectious smile, waiting to jump. She's raising money for charity but that's just an excuse—she's wanted to do it for years. In ten minutes' time, she'll be writhing on the grass after a horrifying landing, her leg broken, her torso developing dark purple bruises. When the local paper runs the story, though, she'll double her sponsorship via their kind-hearted readers.

Max dabs the abrasions dry—

You wince. "Shit!"

"Keep still."

—then wraps a bandage around your foot. You gnaw your sleeve to suppress the urge to pull away. His face is imprinted with diligence and compassion. For a moment you don't know him—he's no more real than the images in the mirror, a glimmer of someone long gone.

You're in black, with a dazed, distressed expression. A funeral. Your father's, just last year. In the mirror, she hasn't cried yet; it's only been a few bleak, hollow days. It'll be several more before reality hits, before she collapses against the lamppost on her way to work, devastated sobs bouncing along the road.

A tear slides down your cheek. Crying even though your doppelganger cannot.

"You can't carry on like this," Max murmurs, making adjustments to the dressing. So far away, you don't realise he's speaking at first.

"Like what?"

He won't answer; he never does. He busies himself with his task, brow furrowed, pinning the bandage securely, tightly. You spot the reflections trying to wriggle free of the pewter frame. Leering and gawping, undeterred. Fingers curl around the edges, salvaging their own versions of reality.

You gasp and squeeze your eyes shut. If you can't see them, they won't see you.

"Sorry," says Max, pulling back.

"No, it wasn't you. I…" You almost explain. You almost blurt out how many versions of yourself are in the room right now, and how they're leaching from the mirror. "It was a wedding present, do you remember?" you say, absently.

One of the counterfeits taunts you with her childish giggles, one stares despondently at an exam paper, one squares up for a fight, while another hides her secrets too well. The one in black gazes into the distance thinking about the hugs she'll never have again. Another freezes in terror in front of her attacker.

A thousand scraps of your forgotten life. A million echoes of the past. All your emotions mustered together. You've been misplacing them for weeks, months maybe, becoming a crumpled cardboard cut-out of yourself, and this is the reason why—they've been drip-dripping into the mirror and now it's overflowing.

You're enchanted by each of the faces, tempted to dive into these other lives, to find one which suits you better. Not your life, not any-more. With each turn, each decision good or bad, these facsimiles have flourished with autonomy and developed possibilities of their own.

The toddler, closed-up and shy, suspicious of people, sits on the pavement with the neighbour's cat in her lap. The cat doesn't want to be here; the girl squeezes him and calls him her 'friend'. He squirms and she doesn't understand why. In a second, he'll scratch her legs and she'll run to her mother howling with shock and a bloody cut on her knee. You have the scar but you're not the child.

"Come on, I'll take you upstairs. You should get some rest."

"No, I need to …" Need to, what? It escapes you.

They're waiting for a moment of weakness. They laugh at your limitations, scoff and sneer, these versions of you who hate you, because you made it, you succeeded. Hate? Such an intense word. It can't be true. Besides, this doesn't feel like success.

The exhausted commuter on the early evening bus focuses on her phone when a track-suited bloke taunts the woman three seats in front with racist slurs—his comments so evidently amusing to him, he reprises them, turning to other passengers and encouraging them to join in. The driver stops, between stops, and hauls him off—a foot taller, a stone heavier.

She should have said something, she should have stood beside the woman and shielded her from the abuse. Instead, it was a dapper white-haired gentleman who checked she was okay, who offered her the handkerchief from his top pocket.

Max sweeps you into his arms the way he once whisked you to bed on languid Sunday afternoons. Today, he barely looks at you.

"Let me go." You writhe against his tight hold.

He restrains you until you succumb with simmering indignation. He carries you upstairs and drops you onto the bed. You undress—rocking your hips left and right, back and forth, easing your trousers towards your ankles, repelling his attempts to help. The slices on your fingers itch. Spots of blood fall onto the white sheets.

Depleted, you slump onto the pillow. Max arranges the duvet, leaving your strapped-up feet uncovered, and kisses your forehead. You want to stroke his cheek or grasp his hand, so he knows you mean thank you. But you can't. You're far-flung and isolated. You are mirror imaged.

Max makes toast—the odour trickles into the walls and floorboards. Poor Max. You never even thought about dinner. The sofa groans when he settles into it; you suspect he does too. The TV blasts out boorishly and the theme tunes from game shows and repeats of *Top Gear* and *Friends* waft up the stairs as he flicks the channels.

He'll ignore the broken mirror. He'll have no regard for the interlopers who will infiltrate the house while you sleep. Or he'll glance anxiously at it and recall what your counsellor said, what the doctors say.

The other versions of you will swarm from room to room, searching, scavenging all your left-over bits. They'll lurk in corners, in the gloom that encircles you. They'll reach out to envelop you, sucking you back. Perhaps a different Kelly would emerge victorious—the one who won her 100-metre sports day sprint, the one who didn't spill coffee on her white shirt on the first day of uni, the one who went to Goa instead of taking a dull, monotonous job because her mother convinced her it was the sensible thing to do. That Kelly might have lived deliberately and remarkably.

Deep into the night, you fight sleep, forcing yourself to stare into the darkness. Your body relaxes despite yourself, immersed into the mattress, cosseted by the duvet. The marauders surround you, murmuring and whispering amongst themselves, placing their hands on you as if *your* existence requires confirmation not theirs.

Max stirs, emitting a soft snore and tugging the covers. The hands vanish; the voices evaporate. Silence swamps you. A cold, flat silence.

You shimmy to the edge of the mattress, extracting yourself from Max's trailing arm. You slide off the bed and press your feet against the floor cautiously. The pain is prickly, like pins-and-needles. The clump of bandages makes walking difficult. You shuffle down the stairs.

The pieces of the mirror aren't where you left them. The beautiful pewter frame is missing, too. Max must have thrown it away after all. You crouch and pat the floor, smoothing your fingertips across the boards. Not a single fragment or stray sliver remains.

You fret they're gone forever, that when you next look into the mirror—any mirror—you won't be there, you'll simply have faded away.

You limp to the kitchen, ignoring the accumulative agony. The only light comes from the clock on the cooker, casting a warm green streak onto the floor, as though you've walked into a witch's coven.

The lid of the bin isn't fully shut, sheets of newspaper peep out. You remove the bundle of yesterday's headlines, unfurling it carefully on the kitchen table. Countless faces look back at you warily, fearful of their future. You sit, relieved to take the weight off your throbbing feet. You lay yourselves out on the table, turning the pieces face up.

You're in your wedding dress, in a barely-there bikini, at a café in Amsterdam, standing beside a waxwork Brad Pitt. You're scowling and smiling and looking surprised. You've got your hands raised in defiance. You're turned towards a sunset. Holding a cocktail glass. Balancing the Eiffel Tower on your palm. You're each of them, all at once.

Of course you are.

Sliding little bits of mirror around, you push the edges together like a jigsaw. There are gaps where pieces have shattered or crumbled, where the curve of a break doesn't quite fit.

It's just you, now; a thousand images of just you, with identical bed-messy hair and shabby dressing gown, and hollow eyes caused by the shadows of green light from the cooker.

These faces are no longer unknown, no longer the enemy; they smile when you smile, they wipe a collective tear from their cheeks. And you piece yourself together because it's what you'll have to do until you can't do it anymore.

CLICK

I watch him leave on the screen of my camera. Click, click, click. With every snap, he's further away; his despondent shuffle exaggerated, his spirit wavering.

I want him to turn, to signal some remorse or anguish at leaving. Or simply to acknowledge I'm here with a comforting glance that says *it's not about you*.

But he doesn't. He keeps his eyes on the pavement, head bowed, shoulders stooped. I imagine him carefully avoiding the cracks, the way we used to together. I wonder if he remembers those prolonged treks to the newsagent when I insisted on returning to some arbitrary point and retracing ourselves because I misstepped.

His hair wafts in the wind, and the low sun turns it a soft auburn. He doesn't check for vehicles as he crosses the road—one car stops abruptly, beeping its annoyance. He waves a brief rebuff and wedges his hands deeper into his pockets.

Click. Click.

If I view though the camera, it's not really happening. It's fiction. I'm seeing a film; I'm staring at an IMAX screen, or at a crisp 1940s black-and-white matinee on BBC2, reassured the end will be happy. I spread my thumb and forefinger across the glass to zoom in. Click.

He's gone. Between that second and the next. Vanishing around the corner. The shape of him remains, the air shimmers like a tarmac mirage in a heatwave. I focus on the point he disappeared, as if the building might shift left and expose him. I imagine him leaning against the wall, his hands hiding his tear-stained face, reluctant to walk away just yet.

I hold my breath. In a moment, he'll race back, sweep me up and twirl me around. One more goodbye. Just you wait. Any second now... Any minute.

Upstairs, my mother weeps. I pull away from my vantage point, turning my head to listen more closely, to discern whether I should go to her. I don't. Her tears alarm me. Mothers shouldn't cry; they should be strong and bold, lionesses guarding their cubs from harm. I step towards the door and pause, unnerved, conflicted by my decision.

Honey and russet leaves fall like confetti. Click. The paperboy cycles past, a whir of legs and wheels. He spots me standing at the window like a ghost. He waves with a cheery grin. Click, click. A soot-black cat stands resolutely in the middle of the road, playing chicken with a four-by-four, scuttling away at the last moment.

"Come away," says Mum in a frail, croaky voice.

She's behind me. Her eyes are raw and puffy, her skin clammy and pale. She's wilting, barely able to lift her head. Her arms criss-cross around her waist; a shawl droops from her shoulders.

The light's fading, the streetlights are coming on. It's past dinner time. It's been hours since he left.

He's not my father. Harry, I mean. My real father left years ago—I barely remember him. Harry appeared when I was ten. Mum introduced him as her friend, a guy who occasionally stopped by with takeaways and Disney DVDs, who began to visit more frequently, bringing sweets and Lego models for us to build together; who was sometimes there at breakfast on a Sunday morning. And I liked him, loved him, in time. He watched my favourite films with me, helped with algebra homework, celebrated exam results with me, bought my first legal pint.

When I imagine getting married, in my far-flung future, it's Harry I picture giving me away.

I was, I mean. Last week, last month.

"He's not coming back, you know," Mum spits out, that day or another. Hours and minutes have drifted into a tangle of resentment. Heartbreak turned to anger.

I stare defiantly, raising the camera to eye level. Her movements are pixelated and stuttering. Click. She scowls, her brow furrows.

Click, click.

Her eyes darken. I scrutinise her through the distance I've created. She snatches for the camera, to steal it from me. I pull my hand away, hiding it behind my back, twisting and turning so she can't reach it. I hold it high, as though it's a game. I laugh, although I don't mean to.

Click, click, click. I back away until I'm on the other side of the room. Her body sags, crumples beneath her, as she concedes defeat. Her energy depleted; her soul crushed. Like mine.

"Fine. Whatever."

"Mum, I…"

She stares, barely noticing me.

"… I'm sorry."

But she walks away.

The unfilled rooms are a harsh reminder. Only now do I notice how much space Harry took up—out there, filling every room he stood in; and in here, in my head, memories detonating when I least want them to. I take refuge behind my lens. It filters the emotions, numbs me, protects me.

Mum's fury has coasted into hopelessness, and melancholy; her pain catches me. I suffer every moment with her. Click. Zoomed in, I capture the inertia and distraction. When I scroll back through, tomorrow or next week, perhaps, I'll see her desperation and grief.

She perches on the edge of the chair, unsure whether she's staying or going. Or she halts half-way up the stairs as though she's lost the volition to go any further. Or she leans against the kitchen sink, or the wall—unsettled, uncertain in her own home. I encounter her staring at a coffee stain on the carpet. Before, she'd have sought out detergents to remove it. She would have scrubbed until it was gone.

"I've ruined everything, haven't I?" she says without looking at me, her voice dull and haunted.

"It wasn't your fault."

Although, I have no idea if it was or wasn't. I'm not meant to. Their increasing antagonism and hostility were concealed from me, kept behind closed doors. Arguments abruptly shut down when I walked into the room, with under-breath mutterings and weighted glances. It hasn't occurred to me to apportion blame.

I withdraw when I see her tears, too real, too inflamed. I don't want real. I want a moment of illusion. I want the pasted-on smiles of my childhood. I zoom out until she's invisible and insignificant within the frame—her minute torso screwed into a ball, long limbs wrapped awkwardly around it.

I can't do anything to help—I don't know where to begin. So, I compile photos, I collate a narrative—a story of the void left behind.

Hours and days melt together. Harry doesn't return, he doesn't phone. He sends a friend to collect his clothes and other belongings, shoving them into the back of his Transit, and I recall he hadn't taken anything with him, that day. I'd hoped it meant he'd come home. Click.

Harry's friend looks abashed when I stand on the stairs watching him battle the front door and two guitar cases. Perhaps I should help. I stand on the stairs, and Mum sits in the living room.

I lose myself in a fervour of assignments. Head down, coffee cold, half-eaten toast at the corner of my desk. It's not the same without Harry there, cheerleading from the side lines, providing chocolate or doughnuts, studying my work as though it's worthy of profound consideration. I hold my camera at arm's length, facing me—click—and set it down without checking the photo I've taken. I don't need to. I know I look wretched.

I turn the music as loud as I dare and lie down on my bedroom floor.

In the kitchen, or the living room, or out in the garden when the sun shines, Mum dances to her own tormented soundtrack. I peer from my window as she hangs the washing. Click. I'm hypnotised by the monotony of her task. For a moment, she stares at the blouse in her hand, as though she's forgotten how to hang it, or why she's doing it.

She's getting thinner. I cook so she doesn't have to and force her to sit at the table with me. Click, click. She doesn't ask me to stop anymore; she doesn't notice. She fills her fork and eats mechanically until the effort has exhausted her enough to give up.

I add filters to make her vintage, then sepia. Layering effects to detach her from herself. I add colour, vivid Warhol highlights; I turn her into an etching. A temporary measure. When I look at her in front of me, she's just as diminished.

She goes to bed at seven and rises for work at six the following morning—I don't see her much. The more she sleeps, the less I do, roaming the house and staring at the TV long after I've lost interest in it. Click. A barren room, rejected and remote. I make snacks that I leave on the side and forget about. I'd never noticed how much Harry held us together, held Mum together. She'd had a hard time when my father left, too, apparently—a spell in hospital while I stayed with my aunt. I don't remember it, but it's not a secret.

Harry knew. And he still left. He must have had a good reason, I decide, though I don't—can't—reconcile that.

I hold my phone to the window and gaze at another frostbitten morning. The black cat stalks across the rickety fences that divide the gardens—click. Our next-door neighbour shuffles to the back lane to retrieve a dustbin—click, click. The last of the leaves die and descend, leaving snarled, knotted branches reaching for the clouds.

I chronicle the sudden snow that blankets the street and makes pavements treacherous; and the ensuing rapid thaw that leaves icy puddles for unsuspecting drivers. Click, click. I wrap myself in a blanket and curl up in the armchair.

Mum dawdles in the kitchen, on Saturday, slow and sluggish, even after all these weeks. She stares out of the window, waiting for her toast, and catches sight of a robin landing on the roof of the shed. She leans against the sink to follow its skip and flutter towards the feeder hanging on next door's tree, fascinated and heartened.

The toaster pops, and Mum grabs her breakfast, buttering it and eating it where she stands. She turns the radio up a little louder and sings along with a couple of lines—silently, just her lips moving between chews. The sun shines, lighting up her face. She looks pretty when she smiles, lost in a memory. I'm motionless in the doorway, not wanting to interrupt.

But I can't help myself—click. I turn and hurry away before she has time to admonish me.

In the living room, I sit on the floor beside the radiator and scroll through my photos, all of them, from the beginning—the day I told Harry I wanted to do photography at college and he bought me a camera. I upload them to my laptop, and he stares right at me; his scruffy grin, his blue eyes dancing as he poses for the shot.

I turn Harry and my mother watercolour and line-drawn and retro. Each filter pushes him away, removing him from the family. The further I distort him, the more my anger dissipates. It's just us now, on my screen, in real life. I blur his features until there's nothing left.

Mum appears, looking past me and peering at the screen—the

64

fully-focused, fortified version of her. She squeezes my shoulder, and her hand remains for a moment, warm and reassuring.

Later, we watch TV together, huddled beneath a fluffy blanket in front of a romantic comedy, pretending not to cry at the saccharine resolution. I hold my camera up—click—for a tear-stained selfie.

"Oh no, don't do that," she says. "Delete it. Delete them all."

But I won't, because she's smiling. She's still pale and burdened, but her vitality is returning. One day, I'll show her how strong she is.

ONE MINUTE SILENCE

This is the way time counts down…

Ten. People go about their business as usual. The front desk manager sits at reception to oversee new arrivals. She attends to a request about room service. Guests mill about, preparing for the day ahead.

Nine. A bride and groom carry boxes of white rose centrepieces and lilac ribbon through the foyer. The maître d' greets them warmly and steels himself for final instructions from the over-zealous bride.

Eight. Upstairs, a guest sits at his dressing table with an open ring binder containing the latest draft of his fourth novel. He twirls a red pen between his fingers and thumb, and reads the first paragraph, over and over, until the words mutate beneath his gaze. He throws the pen across the room.

Seven. A housekeeper rattles her trolley along the corridor on the first floor, moving from room to room—bathrooms cleaned, towels replaced, sides wiped to eliminate dust. She wedges extra teabags into the caddy and counts the packets of sugar.

Six. A woman rushes across the sea front towards the Sea View

Hotel. She's late—her first job interview in weeks, and she's going to blow it. Typical. Her stiletto heel sticks in a crack on the pavement, pitching her forward. "Shit," she mutters, startling a woman walking past her.

Five. The bride and groom sip a complimentary glass of wine, silently considering tomorrow. After months, years—it seems—of planning, they've made it. Nervous and excited, unable to reconcile those contrasting emotions, they smile coyly at each other. A small amount of dread rises between them.

Four. The author doodles little houses in the corner of Page One without taking his pen off the paper. He doesn't remember how to finish off the cross within the square, so he's abandoned each one in various incomplete stages. He skims the first line—again—and grumbles in frustration.

Three. In the ballroom, the maître d' positions the centrepieces on the top table. He brushes the tablecloth with a reverential flick. On the eleven circular tables evenly spaced in front of it, glasses and cutlery are already laid.

Two. The housekeeper turns down the king-size bed in room 112, smoothing and resmoothing to ensure no creases; she plumps the pillows. She straightens bottles of perfume and returns strewn lipsticks to the makeup bag.

One. The interviewee pauses just outside the hotel to compose herself. The author leans back in his chair. The housekeeper stands at the window to open the curtains.

Boom!

Birds stop singing; the wind dies away; even the waves cease their incessant crashing against the rocks.

The seconds afterwards are protracted.

How silent can a town be? Too silent. How much can change all at once? Too much.

*

One moment, the Sea View Hotel is prominent, dominating the sky-line alongside a terrace of Victorian townhouses. The next, there's a vacuum as one whole wing of the hotel bursts across the road.

Fragments of debris hang in the air, as if frozen in time. Everyone holds their breath. Hands are thrown up in fright. Shrieks of warning or shock are unheard; shrieks of horror are caught on the breeze. The abruptness of what's just happened is inexplicable.

From deep inside, the alarms sound. A woman screams from an upstairs window. Faces appear at others, curtains are pushed aside, heads lean out and stare in bewilderment.

A cloud of rubble mushrooms and settles like snow, pattering softly to the ground. The walls teeter precariously. Small groups of tourists gawk at the jagged edges. Furniture from first and second floor bedrooms crash into the ornamental flowerbeds; curtains flap, carpets dangle.

"Fire!" someone shouts, as the first flicker of a flame breaks free.

The spectators scatter, this way and that—some run forward to help, others flee to protect themselves.

Dust-covered people, like zombies, emerge from the hotel, dazed and shielding their eyes from the glare of the pre-noon sun. They wander aimlessly or attempt to go back in to find their friends and loved ones. People limp. People hold their heads or arms as blood seeps from deep gashes. They shiver with shock and hold their hands over their ears to suppress the noise. In slow-motion they slither from the building, gasping for fresh air, and fall gratefully into the arms of strangers who drag them to safety.

Claire—with her interview clothes grimy and ruined—watches aghast, jostled by people running in every direction. She fumbles for her mobile to phone 999, but several people around her are already connected and talking frantically. The hubbub is disorientating.

If she'd been a few minutes earlier, if her heel hadn't snagged on the pavement, she would have been inside already. She gasps and her legs buckle beneath her.

The blaze creeps along the front of the building, from the destroyed ballroom to the small lounge next to it, and up the heavy, plush velvet curtains hanging at every window. Glass shatters. Smoke curls through the gaps.

Claire turns to go; she can't watch anymore.

"Oi, come with me," yells a man in a fluorescent jacket, grabbing her hand. He pulls her back towards the hotel, but she twists away, shaking her head. He points to the floor. "This guy. Stay with him. Don't let him sleep. Please."

Claire looks down at the man groaning and squirming in agony. His arm is broken, horribly twisted with the bone protruding. He's got a red pen clasped in his fist. His eyes are open but glazed and distant. His face is covered with blood; there's a deep cut just above his eye.

The Hi-Vis man dives back into the crowd.

"Wait, I don't know what—"

But he's vanished into the haze. She stares helplessly at the man on the floor, then sits beside him. She removes her jacket and folds it under his head. He mumbles incoherently.

"I'm Claire. What's your name?"

He opens his mouth and winces. It sounds like he says Stuart. He slurs and swallows—the effort of talking is laborious. His breathing is raspy and clumsy. His eyes are closing, fading.

"Hey, Stuart, stay with me. You can't go to sleep. Do you understand? You've got a cut on your head—you need to stay awake. The ambulance'll be here really soon, okay?"

Someone screams out a warning, and Claire ducks as debris from the roof tumbles and bits of brick splatter to the ground. People rush past; she shields Stuart as much as she can. The fire is growing more ferocious inside the building, the roar becoming louder.

"I just need..." he mutters.

"Don't you dare go to sleep. Tell me what you've been doing today. What did you have for breakfast? Stuart, wake up, please."

His face relaxes and softens, the pain diminishing as he drifts into unconsciousness.

More wreckage falls, thudding around them. They can't stay here, it's not safe, but she can't move him alone.

"Help!" Claire cries, plaintively.

No one hears. She surveys the pandemonium. Suffocating black smoke circles the car park. People dawdle in the confusion, bumping into each other—in the way or trying to help, it's hard to tell. Casualties are still emerging, bewildered—people with more serious injuries who've been sought out and rescued by others.

Disembodied voices call from all sides. No one's going to hear her tiny voice in all that.

In room 112, Mavis still has the curtain in her hand. Except, both Mavis and the curtain have been thrown to the opposite side of the room, trussed up together. Part of the floor is caved in, flames are pushing upwards, the floorboards crackle, the carpet is charred and glowing.

"Help!"

Her voice is lost in the clamour of the hotel tumbling. She pushes herself against the wall, grappling for the door handle. But the door's jammed, the wall is twisted. She pulls and pulls, desperately, frantically. Streaks of sweat and sticky tears run down her face, the fire scorches her skin.

"Help!"

Her path to the window is obstructed; there's no way to attract attention, no way for anyone to know she's here. She bangs on the door hysterically. Exhausted, she leans against the moulded wood, staring in horror at the curtains engulfed in flames.

She whimpers. Each breath comes with a peculiar, uncontrollable whine. She trembles. It won't be long before the room is an inferno.

Far away, Mavis hears screams—from outside and above, and all around. Just like the flames.

"Oh God, oh God."

She pulls at the door again, bracing one foot against the frame. It shifts, but not enough. She pauses to recover her strength, then tries again. And again. Until her sixty-year-old limbs are too weak to hold on anymore.

Sirens reverberate through the streets from all four corners of town, battling their way through busy traffic and out to the sea front.

The Sea View aches, weeps, but remains defiant—for now. On the far side of the car park, Charlotte, the duty manager, is rallying her staff who are marshalling bystanders and the walking wounded towards the lawn on the other side of the road. There are people still unaccounted for, but the foyer is besieged by the flames. No one can get in, or out. Stuart and Claire, and small pockets of people just like them, hunker down and wait.

But it's hot, so hot, as the blaze gathers pace. They should move. Should they move? She scans around for help, but there's a dearth of people. Her legs have gone dead from kneeling in one position. She'd never be able to carry Stuart by herself.

A girl in hotel uniform leans against the wall, looking weary and scared. Claire meets her eye and smiles, but the response is muted and hopeless. She listens to the conversations around her, of people reassuring others that help is coming or asking if they've seen Sid or Jessica or any one of the many who are missing.

Smoke pours from the first-floor windows, glass shatters, flames climb onward and upward, casting an orange tinge across the car park. Two people stuck on the third-floor shout—a chilling sound, though they're safe for now. Claire watches the duty manager—the woman she was due to meet with—trying to communicate with the trapped people, using hand gestures.

The fire engines and ambulances take forever, the wailing of the sirens ebbs and flows as they follow the twists of the roads. Mavis, still trapped, closes her eyes and slumps to the floor, her breathing is shallow now, there's not enough air. She prays. She hasn't prayed since she was in school, she doesn't really know what to say.

Claire holds Stuart's hand and whispers, "They're on their way. Can you hear them? I can hear them."

All at once, paramedics and fire crews and police swamp the scene, diffusing into their respective jurisdictions. Their barked instructions supersede everything else. Charlotte relinquishes the authority with gratitude.

Claire scrambles to her feet and waves wildly. "Over here! He's unconscious."

Two paramedics swoop down on them, kneeling beside Stuart, making initial their assessment and firing questions.

"About fifteen minutes… Stuart, I think… I don't know… He didn't say… No, he hasn't…" She bats away tears, frustrated by her ineptness.

They transfer him to a stretcher and carry him cautiously around the many obstacles in their path, past the still-gawking tourists with their cameras and mobiles. Claire follows; she doesn't know what else to do. She hovers at the back of the ambulance while Stuart is tended. He's motionless and grey. Her gaze is drawn to the hotel, to the black smoke pouring from the windows and doors, to the splintering glass falling, to the wounded littering the forecourt.

Somehow she's hauled onto the ambulance, the doors slam shut, and she's whisked off to the hospital with Stuart. She does the only thing she can—she sits next to him and tells him he's going to be okay.

The sirens cease, but the blue lights are still flashing into room 112. The orange flames climb the curtains. Wallpaper peels, paint bubbles, the ceiling bows hazardously. Mavis tucks her legs towards her, until her knees are wedged into her chest.

The yelling now is from the fire brigade who are unfurling hoses and preparing to fight the seat of the fire. Mavis turns her head as water starts to surge into the room—they're aiming at the ground floor, but the spray is permeating upwards. Mavis feels the mist on her skin, cooling her, dampening her clothes, providing relief and an extra layer of protection. She chokes as the foul smoke billows around the room.

Floorboards buckle. Another piece of the room falls to the ground.

The first body is found while the hotel still burns. A firefighter yells out, with his hand in the air, to prevent his colleagues from trampling over him—a sombre moment that they were gloomily prepared for. He's discovered on a bed of lilac tablecloths and white roses. Michael Dorries, of twelve years' impeccable service at the Sea View Hotel, is carried from the hotel in a black body bag and along a line of police officers who are shielding him from the onlookers.

Somewhere across town, Mrs Dorries has no idea her husband is in that bag. She won't find out for another hour. It's Charlotte's duty to unofficially identify him, to be the first to mourn him. She feels sick. She shivers and can't stop. She watches his body sliding into the ambulance, reaching out to touch the door as it drives away. Her hand remains lost in the air. She turns and stares dejectedly at the destruction, and the persistent fire still crawling onwards.

The hotel is battered; its windows warped and doors charred with the impression of flames. It creaks and groans.

A large chunk of masonry falls. Charlotte holds her breath, too late to shout out. Several people leap out of its path.

She gazes at the shattered lump and runs her hand through her hair. The chief fire officer tries to explain the extent of the operation. She's traumatised and confused—watching his lips moving but with little comprehension.

The hotel teeters—walls bulge, floors cave and droop. A booming crash on the far side reverberates through adjacent side-streets. People gasp. Some take pictures. It'll be all over social media within minutes.

Last week, the Sea View was an eyesore. There was a dilapidated drabness, a melancholy feel. The edges were frayed; the original sash windows were flaking. Inside, the carpets were shabby and stained, the upholstery faded. It was a remnant of a bygone era. Around it stood—stands, will stand—new glass-fronted buildings, bright and proud, displacing it even more.

But it belonged. It fitted. It was the town's remnant, the town's history. It opened in 1845, the grandest hotel in the area, the most beautiful building by far. Queen Victoria spent a night here, and her portrait hangs—hung, will never hang again—in the wide, elaborate staircase.

With the wealth of graduations and weddings and birthdays hosted here, almost everyone who lives in the town has been inside the Sea View at one time or another. And because of that, an opaque grief descends as news spreads.

More people arrive to witness the devastation for themselves. A vague, hushed murmur drifts over the crowd. People are in awe as it sizzles and cracks, standing in silence to watch it burn.

Mavis is kneeling, face low eking out the last bit of oxygen, her mouth covered with a damp towel from the ensuite. She can hear footsteps coming closer. She bangs on the door. "Help. I'm in here. I'm stuck. Help."

She presses her ear to the door and feels the penetrating heat on the side of her face. She bangs again but no one comes. She forces her whole body into the wall, the advancing heat licking her.

Bang, bang, bang. "Hello?" says a deep voice, and Mavis lets out a cry, a sob of joy.

Tears stream down her face as the door is finally beaten down. The black smoke is sucked away. The corridor is cooler, the air marginally clearer, a reprieve. She takes deep breaths which make her dizzy. She's swept her off her feet and carried away, emerging into daylight.

Mavis is absorbed into the arms of her husband, who arrived as soon as he could after he heard the news on the radio. He hugs her as though he'll never let her go. She nuzzles her face in his chest to avoid the distress around her.

Claire lights a cigarette outside the hospital in the neighbouring city, looking towards the coast. The black plume has flattened and hovers like a cloak. It starts to dissipate as the wind catches it, creating the shape of elephants and spaceships and castles. The fire must be out.

You can't see the hotel from here—the city falls away into a wide, shallow valley, with rows of grey roofs in long straight lines, before climbing out the other side and forming the outskirts of the coastal town. She wonders what the sea front looks like now, how odd it will be to walk up there tomorrow, or the next day.

If she were closer, she'd smell the acrid air, she'd feel the heat. If she were closer, she'd see the space where the hotel was. She'd see subdued search parties scrambling through scorched debris, hunting for people still lost. She'd hear the haunting sound of embers crackling and sizzling.

She takes a final drag and stubs the cigarette out, while tilting her head back and blowing smoke into the air. She doesn't want to go back inside, she's superfluous. She peers through the glass doors and watches the bustle of A&E—most of the hotel casualties are here, their smoky stench fills the air. She hasn't properly explained she isn't Stuart's girlfriend—but *he* will, as soon as he wakes up. She shouldn't be here then, to be called out as a fraud or some weird kind of stalker.

But they still don't know who Stuart is. All the things with his name on are under a pile of rubble—either in his room or on the register in the damaged reception. Somewhere, elsewhere, he's got a wife or girlfriend, kids maybe, definitely parents who have no idea he's injured. He's shipwrecked and alone but doesn't yet realise it. She can't leave him like this, can she?

75

Claire reaches into her pocket for another cigarette, then realises what she's doing and stops. She should be quitting, but it's been a stressful day. She'd already got herself worked up about the interview, she couldn't imagine it would end like this. She drags herself back into the hospital and sits in the waiting room. She shouldn't be here.

Time slows down; the clear up begins.

The townspeople are lured to the saturated wreck, unable to draw themselves away, sombre and curious, hypnotised by the smouldering ruin. They bring bouquets of vibrant flowers to disguise the pain and notes of sympathy for the three fatalities they never knew.

The one-minute silence happens by accident. Because that's what happens after a tragedy, after people have died. People in shock say nothing, do nothing. They congregate, finding solace in the presence of others. The firefighters and police bow their heads and the crowd follows. The only sound is from the wind and the waves. As twilight falls, a grey mist descends.

Someone coughs, another sniffs. Someone else hums awkwardly. A siren wails along a street on the way to a new emergency, echoing around the two- and three-storey buildings of the town centre. A motorbike growls along the sea road and makes several people jump; seagulls squawk overhead.

Gradually these sounds fade away, they fracture, and silence pulses through the gathering: its fingers wrap around them and draw them together.

It's harrowing to see the Sea View crushed. Charlotte is empty, devastated as she recalls arriving at work yesterday, walking up those imposing steps and through the large front door.

The bride is inconsolable, hanging onto her groom's arm, her face mottled, and her eyes swollen. She tries her best to think of the people who died, the people severely injured—but her grief returns to her non-wedding tomorrow.

People turn inward—they think of their graduation ceremony so many years ago, or the Christmas party from last year. They think of loss, of their friends and family no longer with them. They listen to the waves crashing, to the wind rushing towards them—they hear the music, they sway together.

A whistle blows to mark the end. A murmur ripples through them. People breathe deeply and pretend they weren't shedding a tear. No one seems to know what to do next. They remain, holding vigil or simply too scared to go in case the whole building crumbles while they're not looking. But the weather turns, the rain comes in droves, and gradually the sea road is vacated. Grey puddles form.

This is the way time passes.

One. An eerie hollowness takes over. The blanket of flowers turns to mush in the ensuing stormy weather. Metal barriers are erected around the site, signs warning against trespassers are displayed.

Two. Stuart is sitting up in his hospital bed, his arm set, his head bandaged. (His novel is a wreck—the handwritten edits are missing —and he considers abandoning it altogether.) Claire slipped away when his wife, who'd driven three hundred miles through the night to be with him, arrived. At home, she throws her clothes into the washing machine and pours herself a glass of wine. And she sobs, alone in her flat, as the reality of the past couple of days sinks in.

Three. The gap in the skyline draws the eye. It's a glaring over-sight, as though a child has covered the hotel with their fist, the way they would hold the sun between their finger and thumb, an optical illusion. When you walk past, the space hits your peripheral vision, a startling white hole.

Four. The hotel staff hold a farewell party, for the hotel, for their deceased colleagues, for themselves. It won't re-open, so they'll go their separate ways. Mavis is retiring—her husband already has— and they're moving close to their daughter in Kent. She hates the idea of leaving town but can't bear the memories.

Five. People slow down as they walk past, paying their respects, being nosey. They recall the day it happened and are either upset they witnessed it or regretful they didn't. There's a lingering gloom, an unshakeable sorrow, a collective lament.

Six. Graffiti appears, random swear words are spray-painted onto the side of the building. Someone thinks it's funny to draw flames. Over time, the windows that were left intact are broken by stones thrown from the pavement. Elderly ladies tut, claiming to have never seen such disrespect.

Seven. An inquest concludes that a gas leak was ignited by a light switch in the corridor between the kitchen and ballroom. Commuters read the report in the Recorder with mild interest and leave the paper on the seat when they alight the bus. The next person reads, and discards.

Eight. Weeds curl around the crumbling walls and creep across the floor of the foyer and dining room; tall yellow flowers spring up, growing denser. The space seems almost too small for the grand building that once filled the spot.

Nine. The town celebrates Christmas with a fayre; the lights are switched on by a minor local celebrity. Everyone enjoys the dramatic fireworks with their backs towards the derelict site.

Ten. People's memories are short. They go about their business, as usual.

BLACK DOG

I have a black dog. With bottomless brown eyes that impede me wherever I go and ears that prick at every unexpected noise. He rests his head in my lap to remind me he's there and nuzzles against my leg. Sleek, majestic, wily.

When I shower, or take the bins out, or shovel laundry into the washing machine, his nose is rammed against my hand, manoeuvring me to focus on him. He almost purrs.

Yet once I've patted him, and said Good Boy, he won't quit. He nudges my hand, pushing upwards when I'm carrying hot drinks. He nips my calves to hurry me along or slow me to a torpid crawl. He whines and yaps in aggravated bursts; a constant reverberation in my head.

My black dog lumbers around the house, flopping onto the floor to trip me when I try to cross the room, burying my blister-packed medication in the garden, thwarting my enervated attempts to do anything at all. A stubborn weight sitting on my chest.

We go for walks, my dog and I, just to get some peace. He sprints for sticks and chases squirrels up trees. We frolic feverishly through parks and streams and along the lanes that circle our town. Sometimes there are not enough places to be. No matter how many hours we're out, he's still bouncing off the walls when we return while I lie down, exhausted, and can barely feel my limbs.

Alert all day, howling all night. An incessant drone drilling my skull. I sneak off without him, hiding behind shrubs and fences for a moment's peace, holding my breath in case he can sense me with his acute intuition. He is not fooled. He hunts me down like it's a game. Sitting and waiting, his head cocked to one side.

Abruptly, for days or weeks at a time, he coils motionlessly into a snug circle, nose tucked beneath his tail, and snores like a mollified baby; but the serenity is tentative, and I wait for the fracture.

THE FEAR OF GHOSTS

I fumble at the front door for the doorbell, a rusty handle set into the eroding stone archway. My fingers curl around the rusted metal. It's stiff; I imagine it hasn't been used in a long time. I pause, steeling myself. I don't have to be here; I could turn around and go home. She'd never know.

Except the taxi pulls away, crunching along the gravel driveway and out onto the main road. I swallow as I listen to it purr into the distance. My heart misses a beat. I yank the handle, and a bell jangles inside the house.

The doctor said he'd be here. He said he'd been staying since my mother got worse a few days ago; one of the perks of having a friend as your family doctor, I suppose. It should have been me, of course, tending to her, providing comfort in what might be her final hours. But I put off visiting for as long as possible. Now, it's almost too late.

"Michael, it's good to see you." Jack grabs my hand and shakes it. His fingers are sharp, his skin papery. He's got old. I pull away quickly.

"Doctor Jack," I say, with a slight bow.

It's what I called him when I was a child and he was newly arrived in our one-track village.

He chuckles. "Come in, come in."

Stale air creeps towards me. A cold breath brushes the back of my neck. I hear the whispers. I wince.

Jack takes my bag and places my hand on his out-stretched arm. He guides me into the house. I scuff my feet on the thick carpet, and he holds his hand against my chest to steady me. "Okay? We'll go into the drawing room—it's warm in there. Turn left."

"I know the way."

He ignores me. "Two more steps, that's it. You're in front of an armchair."

He allows me to turn and touch the chair with the back of my legs. I hesitate, unable to catch my breath. The room sucks the oxygen away from me. I take a deep gulp.

"Are you all right?"

"Yes. Yes, of course."

"Under the circumstances."

"Indeed." I perch on the edge of the chair, stiff and straight-backed—both the chair and me. "How is…?"

A bell rings from upstairs.

"Excuse me—your mother calls." He exits, mumbling how he wished he'd never given her the bloody thing. I laugh softly.

The room is noisy without him. The steady ticking of a clock; the crackle of logs on the fire and an unexpected clunk as one settles; the screech of a shrub scraping against the window. I scratch at the threadbare arms of the chair with my too-long fingernails. I prise my hands away, and my fingers curl around themselves instead, scratching at skin.

The house hasn't changed, this room certainly hasn't. The air is oppressive and musty; my mother has always insisted the curtains are kept closed to block out draughts. It has a waning smell of beeswax polish and burned candlewick. It will still be cluttered and claustrophobic, the over-sized walnut furniture—tall dressers, chairs and side tables—all squeezed together.

And the cabinet. Of course. I'd forgotten about it—how strange.

That robust, foreboding cabinet; that bristle in the air.

I tremble. I'm nine again, petrified. Under my bed, with my fist shoved into my mouth to prevent me from making a noise. Running away, only to be thwarted at every ornately carved doorway or overfurnished landing. Calling for help, but my voice too feeble; and my parents assuming I'm playing a game, anyway—admonishing me for disturbing them.

My body rigid, my feet pushing into the carpet to anchor myself. They're coming, prowling; their icy fingers reaching out…

The ghosts.

The sound of my mother's bedroom door closing echoes into the large hallway.

How did I forget the ghosts?

They draw back into their closet confinement, and I breathe again. I smirk at my foolishness. I'm safe, of course; I'm an adult and my nightmares can't harm me anymore.

I trace Jack's journey down the stairs and into the drawing room. "She's hanging on," he says. He pauses in the middle of the room, to stretch perhaps, to rock his head from side to side and alleviate the stress. "She's a resilient woman."

"Yes, she is."

"Would you like a drink? It's been a long day, I could use one." He sounds drained and defeated. I should have come sooner.

I shake my head. "Is this it, Jack? Is she…?"

"She's been ill for a long time. She's lucky to have made it this far, to be honest." He's at the sideboard, chinking the decanter— whiskey, maybe—against two glasses, even though I said no. A cube of ice is dropped in each one.

"I didn't realise. I'd have been here if…"

If what? If I'd known? If I'd had nothing better to do?

"I know. But she wouldn't let me tell you how bad things really were. A strange decision, but..." He presses a glass into my hand. "Here. Drink. Doctor's orders."

The cabinet was in my bedroom at first, storing disregarded and neglected toys. An aunt I never met left it to my parents in her Will. There wasn't space for it anywhere else, so it was left in my room.

It gave me nightmares, looming over me as I slept, forcing me to hide under the scratchy woollen blankets. I'd peek out periodically, to catch the ghosts as they evaporated into the darkness.

"It's been in the family for years," my mother said as I stared up with trepidation. Up and up and up.

I told her about the nightmares.

"Don't be silly. It's just a cupboard." Dismissing me with a brief flick of her hand.

"It moves when I'm sleeping!" I called as she withdrew.

She didn't tell me—and I didn't find out until later—that each of its previous owners had suffered ruin and torment. Houses razed to the ground, ancestors found guilty of treason and hanged, or crushed and mutilated by a horse and cart, or blown off cliffs and drowned. One poor woman was tried as a witch and burnt. Family folklore blamed the cabinet for it all.

The ghosts were tentative at first; prodding me, analysing me. Testing me. It *was* a game; a weapon I could use against my parents. But they grew stronger, and they made me weaker. They bullied and taunted me; intimidated me, terrified me.

Even when it was brought down into this room, the ghosts didn't let go. Seeking me out, clinging to me, invading me. I tried to fight back, but they always beat me. Occasionally, I felt an extra strength sustaining me when I couldn't stand anymore, another presence to line up beside me.

But it didn't work. I got sick. They made me sick.

My parents never hid their disappointment in me. They'd had high hopes for their only child: Head Boy, captain of the cricket team, Cambridge, a career in law or banking. Instead, I told them ghost stories and withered away. Some days, I could barely leave my room. They paid for the best doctors, but no one could tell them what was wrong with me.

The day I left home, for boarding school aged ten, I recovered. The fog of infirmity lifted. I never went back.

I have a good life now: a job I enjoy, close friends, occasional girl-friends who come and go by mutual agreement. I didn't ever want to return to this house. I put it off as long as possible.

"How have you been?" Jack asks, in a tone which suggests it isn't his first attempt to break my ruminations.

"Good."

"You look well. London life agrees with you."

"This house has a habit of dragging me down."

"Ah yes, your tales of ghosts." He chuckles. "I remember them well."

I nod guardedly. *Yes, tales.* My fingers follow the intricate pattern etched into the crystal tumbler. "Did my mother ever explain it to you, why she sent me away?" I swig the remainder of my drink. I regret asking; I don't really want to know. It was my salvation, after all. I should be grateful.

Jack sucks air, and shuffles in his chair. It creaks as he leans forward and his glass thuds onto a coaster on the side table. I imagine his elbows resting on his knees and his fingers pressed together—his signature pose, the stern doctor persona that used to frighten me into taking my medication.

"She said she had no choice. Her grief was too severe, and you needed so much care." He pauses, stumbling over his words.

In my mind, he's perspiring copiously, mopping his brow with a handkerchief from his jacket pocket. Or perhaps I'm just recalling films my mother used to watch. There was always a lot of brow-mopping in those.

"She couldn't cope on her own," he continues, faintly. "Do you remember how she took to her bed and refused to leave?"

"No."

"No… well, you were recovering from your own injuries…" The ticking clock infiltrates the room. "She said… she said you reminded her too much of your father."

"Oh."

"It's my fault. I should have done more. I should have saved him." His voice is blunted, caught in his throat.

"You did everything you could."

There was a fire. I was trapped in my bedroom. I screamed from the window, so very scared, but no one came. It felt like hours, but finally, standing in the doorway, my father held out his arms and I stumbled into them. He hugged me close and struggled through the furious fire. Part of the ceiling crashed on top of us. We scrambled out, bleeding and concussed, battling to the door. I couldn't see through the thick smoke. It attacked my throat and eyes; I choked and convulsed, clutching onto him. He collapsed onto the lawn, and I was blind.

I blamed the ghosts, but nobody listened.

The doctor and I sit in silence, contemplating how that one event changed so much.

"Are you ready to see her?" Jack asks.

I tilt my head towards the ceiling. "I don't think I'll ever be ready."

A hideous gargling cry emanates from above. Jack rushes from the room, calling out to her as he bounds up the stairs. I stand but make no attempt to follow. I listen closely. The floorboards groan as he moves around the room, urgently at first, with purpose. Then calmer, slower.

He'll bow his head respectfully and cover her with the crisp cotton sheet. I sit heavily and wipe a tear from my cheek.

There are no sounds. Nothing at all. Is that possible? The wind diminishes, the fire ceases its relentless crackling, and even the clock has retreated. As though a shroud has been thrown over me to block everything out.

"I'm sorry, Michael," says Jack, on his return. His appearance is sudden, and I flinch. "It was her time. I held her hand and she passed peacefully."

"Thank you." I should say something further, but I'm numb. I struggle over the words, then give up. I've had time to consider this moment, but it's nothing like I envisioned. I'm hollow, remorseful, ashamed. "What will happen to … um, to her now?"

"I'll send for the undertakers."

"Thank you."

"What about you? Can I give you a lift to the station?"

"I planned to stay for a couple of days." It seemed like a good idea, at the time. I'd assumed Jack would be here, that my mother would hold on for a while longer.

"I should stay with you. You'll need help—you don't know your way around."

"I'll be fine. You should get back to your wife. You've been away long enough. Thank you, for everything."

Doctor Jack ambles around the house, collecting all the things people habitually deposit when then stay anywhere for a length of time, making your house their own—toothbrush, nightwear, medical bag. With a firm handshake, his leaving seems so final.

I don't go to my mother, and I remain in the drawing room when, an hour later, the undertakers come to collect her.

The atmosphere alters immediately. I am chilled. A draught curls around my legs as though the door has been left open. A voice laughs softly.

"So," I mutter, "it's just you and me now."

The ghosts and me.

They don't reply. Of course they don't. Because ghosts aren't real. They're a construct of my childhood imagination.

I rise and totter towards the dresser to top up my drink. Jack was right. I don't know my way around this house anymore—I haven't been here for many years. I visualise perfectly how it used to be, but over time my mother has reduced the number of rooms she uses, squeezing her favourite furniture around her while other rooms stand practically empty. As Jack walked around the house, I could hear the varying concentrations of timbre.

I snag my shin on a low table and alter direction. When I arrived, Jack settled me into the closest chair, but now, traversing the room, I have obstacles. I reach to my left and stroke the curtains to align myself. I turn slightly, pointing myself into the corner where Jack filled our glasses. Procuring a drink shouldn't be this hard, surely.

I grope my way across and grab the dresser with relief.

No. Not the dresser. The Cabinet.

I lean close and breathe in the warm aroma of my childhood. A conflictingly comforting scent of linseed oil, of citrus, of the walnut itself. I press my forehead against it and listen. If they're inside, if they're real, then I'll hear them.

My chest tightens, my heart races. My fingers trace the beading and the detail carved in the wood.

"There are no ghosts. There are no ghosts," I whisper, recalling my childhood, my isolation and abandonment; recalling that the only constant was my fear of them.

I locate the bronze handles, smooth and worn after centuries of use. And I pull. The doors are stiff and open abruptly, creaking on their hinges. I hold my hands up to defend myself.

Nothing happens.

No ghosts. I laugh at myself, a harsh acerbic laugh. No ghosts. Of course not! Stupid man. My nightmares, my juvenile anxiety, it was all in my head. The fire that killed my father was just an accident. The illnesses I suffered, merely unfortunate.

I relax—my shoulders, my arms, my fists. The knot inhabiting my stomach unfurls.

Now what? For so many years, the ghosts filled my head, my fear of them pushed me away, my spite for them drove me forward. It was all a lie. I pat the cabinet the way I acknowledge an old friend. Time for that drink.

Gently, at first, I feel a soft tug. I brush myself down, in case my trouser leg has caught on a splintered corner. I take a step, but still I'm unable to move.

A sharp icy finger strokes my arm. A malformed hand wraps itself around my torso.

The sensation becomes stronger, more urgent, pulling me. I try to resist. I grab the nearest piece of furniture, a table, to secure myself.

A bright light burns my eyes; distorted and muffled yet intensely painful. I can't move. It overwhelms me. I'm transfixed as it refines into a piercing point. I'm drawn to it, towards the cabinet. I wriggle away. I must resist, must be stronger than them. I'm losing my grip. The light magnifies, enveloping me.

The voices rise again, like before. Coaxing me, urging me. Telling me what to do. Soft, gentle, cutting, stark. They've been waiting for this, for me to let down my guard. I'm the child who got away, the last of the family line.

Closer and closer. The wood vibrates—energy restoring, seizing upon my fear, as it did in my childhood imaginings. The evil within calls to me; the voices of my ancestors beseech me to join them— the witches and monsters lurking down the centuries. The noise is incessant and confusing.

"Stop!"

I reach behind me, fumbling for something I can smash down onto the cabinet to break the spell. I find a lamp with a solid metal base. I lift it to test its weight, then raise it above my head and crash it down to splinter the wood.

The cabinet shrieks, high-pitched and mournful. It rings around the room, resonating against the high ceiling, sending a spasm down my spine.

I'm jolted, pushed, dragged towards the gaping doors. Arms lift me and throw me to the floor. My head is heavy. I wipe my forehead and discover blood. Everything is foggy and clouded. I can't… think straight. I try to remember where I am, what I'm doing.

The cabinet!

I haul myself to my feet, and lift the lamp again, smashing it down onto the ghosts over and over. I'm shoved against the wall, winded, grappling for breath. I punch the air, trying to fight, but how can you attack something that doesn't exist? I surge forward with a yell, and the resistance evaporates. I fall again, bumping into the corner of the dresser or a table.

For a moment, I'm warm and embraced. I don't want to move. I want to remain here. The throb in my head gradually dissipates. I'm drowsy, comfortable.

A hand snakes around my throat and tightens. I can't breathe. I see my mother and father, young and smiling at me, holding their hands out to me. I'm running through the long grass in the fields beside our house. I see us all laughing and happy, so happy.

That's what they took, the ghosts. They stole my childhood, and my father; they made my mother old and bitter.

I lash out in rage, but hit nothing, of course. Ghosts aren't real. My parents said so. Jack said so. The hands around my neck are now squeezing my entire body, constricting me, purging the oxygen from me.

The air stagnates. I squirm, but I'm pinned down, paralysed. And the ghosts laugh. Arrogant and scathing in their victory. There's a sharp pain, a trickle of blood down my face. I close my eyes, and my inert body is dragged along the thick shag carpet.

Silence.

At last.

And then…

…the whispering…

…begins again.

Voice upon voice, unspecified and indistinct. My ancient family lineage, welcoming me like a long-lost son. Claiming me as theirs.

The smooth antique Walnut imprisons me, holding me firmly within its layers. I scratch against the grain, searching for a way out; but the wood creaks, and contracts to restrain me further. My limbs seize until they are rigid. I try to squirm away, but I'm trapped.

Exhausted, I allow myself to drift among the molecules and atoms, assimilated.

I hear the narratives of my ancestors—their stories of witchcraft and chaos, of malevolence and domination. I see the cabinet passed from generation to generation, stealing kin from the outside world, as though I'm living through it. A collage of images, like memories, passing through me.

But what now? There's no more family. I'm the last of the line.

We'll start again, of course. The cabinet will be purchased from a second-hand shop, nestled alongside all the other furniture from my mother's house. We'll be inserted into a new home, loved and admired. We'll whisper tenderly, affectionately, and a child will hear us, the youngest and the weakest. Like me.

ADVENTURES IN MY
OWN BACK GARDEN

My back garden is a sanctuary because the world is too big. When I stare from my bedroom window, I'm struck by the stillness, by my own serenity. The patio doors are open, and a breeze drifts into the room; the smell of cut grass mingles with furniture polish and bacon sizzling in the kitchen. I glide into the back garden, with its high stone walls and neat bed of roses. A tree growing tall in next door's garden bends towards me.

I gaze at the deep blue sky and imagine diving into it, like a cold lake on a hot summer's day. I feel my arms and legs slicing through it, catching gulps of untainted air from high up in the atmosphere. I corkscrew with the currents, pirouetting until I can't tell which way is up; my torso lithe and dexterous, splashing through the clouds.

Of course, I'm not swimming, or flying for that matter. I didn't swim for years before the accident, and now I never will. One more of those things I took for granted as a kid—like skateboarding and cycling and rolling from the top of a grassy slope—stolen from me.

My limbs are extraneous—loose threads leftover.

There was a relentlessly cheerful physio at the hospital who cajoled me to push against her hand, who praised every perceived attempt. I wasn't doing anything, there was no force on her whatsoever, even though my brain was assuring me my effort was at eleven.

She didn't react when I growled my frustration. She simply held a beaker of water and propped my head at such an angle I could sip through the straw. She distracted me by talking about the weekend's football scores until I was recovered enough to try again.

She was cute. I'd wanted to show her how amazing I was, how my ability to move her hand backwards, just a little, was indicative of what a great boyfriend I'd make. I'm pretty sure she had a crush on me, too.

The silence in my garden is a relief, after many months in hospital with its daily routines, frequent dramas, and persistent bustle. Being alone is soothing. The sky is infinite.

***

My back garden is a window. Beyond the wall at the end of the garden is a service lane that connects one road to another, and on the other side are the back gardens of the houses on the next road over. Kids use it as a shortcut to school, shouting and yelling just for the sake of it, the way kids do. It makes me anxious when I hear them; my fear emanates as a low-pitched whine that I can't control.

There's one lad who leaps up every morning, waving his hands over the top of the wall as though he knows I'll be there to see him. I've never seen his face—he's not tall enough, and by the time he is, he'll be at the secondary school in the other direction.

I see the heads of their parents, bobbing along as if disconnected from their bodies. Like me. Floating heads going about their daily business perfectly normally. They talk loudly to each other, batting pleasantries back and forth. And sometimes they're on their phones, so there's no *back* part of the conversation, leaving me unfulfilled and curious.

From the window, I witness the seasons changing. It's late spring —the trees are forcing out new green leaves, and birds are tweeting from dawn to dusk while my mother throws her slipper at them. She's lost three already this year. This latest one catches on a branch.

"I see you laughing, Stephen," she calls in mock chastisement, and we both focus on the pale lilac addition to next door's apple tree. She disappears into the shed and emerges with a broom—I assume she's going to stage a rescue attempt.

I'm out here most days when the weather's fine. I don't get much choice, of course, but I like the warmth of the sun on my face, the sound of traffic humming on the main roads that snake around my house, the occasional helicopter whirring overhead.

Today, from one of the neighbour's open windows, the sound of piano floats through the gardens—it's a beautiful melody, a sound-track to the tranquillity of my life. I sway in time with the music. I *imagine* I'm swaying.

***

My back garden is a cage. Mum brings me outside every day, and I'm presumed to be grateful. At regular intervals she moves me to the left so I remain in the shade, or she turns me so I have something different to look at; or she brings water; or sits with me and tells me about the vacuum cleaner which is making that funny noise again. I'm supposed to be grateful, not petulant.

"Fresh air is good for you," she says, knowing I can't answer back or refute her claim.

Or sometimes, she says, with a sigh, "I'm sorry I can't take you out properly. I can't manoeuvre your chair very well. You know that, right? I would if I could…" She'll kneel down and rest her head on my chest, sniffing away a tear.

I breathe in her flowery perfume, and I'm a child again, being tucked into bed before she hosts a dinner party downstairs. When she pulls away, wiping her eyes and trying her best to smile brightly, she looks overwhelmed. And I long to tell her I am grateful and not at all petulant. I want to hug her or hold her hand.

It could be worse. Everyone says so. Not to me, of course, but to Mum, as though this in some way comforts her. Acquaintances commiserate with her, then go home to their husbands and 'perfect' off-spring.

Being out here, in a garden that's getting smaller by the day, is a tease. It invites me to want more—to dash to the end and fling open the wooden gate and stand on the cusp of unaccustomed freedom. I want to step beyond the confines of my house.

***

My back garden is a prison. I wake from a dream, enraged and resentful. I don't remember the dream, just the residual sensations, the injustice, the trepidation. It smothers me, grasps me by the throat and strangles me.

My mother potters around the garden, crouching to reach weeds growing between her beloved roses, removing those tiny innocuous plants designated weeds simply for growing in the wrong place at the wrong time. If this patch of land was a nature reserve, all living things would be valued, nothing would be considered in the way or outstaying their welcome.

I wonder whether I'm a weed too, something my mother would remove if she could. After all, I'm in the wrong place, in the way, taking up room. I returned unannounced, after leaving home and creating a new life for myself, because there was nowhere else for me to go. She probably never envisaged an accident, or the need to care for a paralysed grown-up son.

All our dreams thwarted at once.

Kids walking to school, the helicopter overhead, even the sound of the piano, remind me of all the things I can't do, will never do again.

It's too late to be vengeful or morose or fearful. Shit happens, say bumper stickers across America. In Britain, we have the phrase on badges. We shrug and move on.

I was twenty-eight when my fledgling adulthood ground to a halt. I'd wanted to travel, to get married and have kids. Normal stuff, nothing wild. I didn't even get to pay off my student loan.

I wonder what Mum wanted for her life. I never asked when I could. I'm not sure I cared; I assumed I was her whole world, that everything she did was for my benefit alone. She's sitting on the grass now, leaning against the wall, sipping a glass of water. She has a sheen of sweat and a smear of soil across her cheek. She looks beautiful and content and pensive. She catches my eye and, after a moment, smiles.

***

My back garden is a stage, and I'm the audience.

A ball bounces over the wall from next door, from off-stage. I watch it roll, then settle into a dint in the grass.

"Oi, mate," calls a voice immediately. "Pass the ball back."

I was expecting it to be a kid, or a kid's mother. But this is the tone of a man, deep and gruff, the way mine used to be.

"Mate? Pass the ball, please?"

I stare at the ball with interest. Well, I would if I could. Wouldn't this be an awesome time to develop telekinesis powers? If I could hold the ball steady in mid-air and with a brief flick of my thoughts, launch it back to him? How freaky would that be! I concentrate, but nothing happens.

A head appears. Eyes focus first on the ball, then on me, then on my chair. The smile falls from his face. "Oh, shit. Sorry, mate, I didn't realise." He glances around, then peers over the wall to the patch of grass directly beneath it. "Do you mind?" He makes a gesture, miming jumping over the wall.

I'm blank, curious, but unable to reply. People don't often want to come near me. They garble excuses, or just let their voice drift off when they realise they'll get nothing from me. They shuffle away, red-faced and avoiding eye-contact. I feel sorry for Mum—she puts on her strong face, but she cries at night, in her room, when she thinks I'm asleep.

This man doesn't back away; he wants his ball back after all. He leans on the wall with one hand and springs over, like they do in films when they're trying to outrun the bad guy.

He pauses to compose himself, then side-steps across to the ball, facing me the whole time.

"I'm, er, practising keepie-uppies." He looks embarrassed and passes the ball from one hand to the other. "I work from home, and I procrastinate"—he holds up the ball and grins—"a lot, apparently. I keep a record of how many I've done. Is that weird? I'm on seven hundred and twenty-six, now. In total, not just today."

He pauses again, standing in the middle of a stranger's garden, chatting easily. For all he knows he might be prattling away to someone who can't understand a single word he's saying. I kind of like him for that.

I wonder what he'll do next. He looks up abruptly. "Oh, hi."

"Can I help you?" says Mum, with her stern, protective voice.

"Hi," he says again. "I just came to get my ball. I live next door." He hesitates and tucks the ball under his left arm, offering his right hand to Mum. "I'm Jamie. We've just moved in, me and Rachel, my girlfriend."

"Oh, right." She shakes his hand, with uncertainty.

"We've just been getting to know each other…" He waves his hand towards me.

"This is Stephen." Still wary, her hand squeezes my shoulder.

"Great. Hi, Stephen." He steps forward and touches my hand, a handshake of sorts, I guess. "I'd better go. But I'll see you round, yeah?"

He half-waves at us, then bounces back over the wall. Mum goes back into the house, and I'm alone again.

***

My back garden is a playground. Recently, when I'm out here and Jamie's playing in his, he jumps over the wall to keep me company. He brings his ball and dribbles it around me.

I'm not sure how long it's been since I met Jamie—days or weeks, definitely not months. The weather is drier and becoming warmer. When Mum wheels me outside now, she no longer wraps a blanket around my knees, she puts a baseball cap on my head.

Jamie laughs when he sees me wearing it. "It covers your bald spot."

It's a good job I'm not vain. I used to have long blond hair that fell as a scruffy, curly mess. When I worked at a bar during my degree course, people mistook me for Australian. I'm not sure how I feel about having a bald spot.

Sometimes, Mum brings Jamie a coffee or cold drink and sits with us for a little bit. She constantly asks if he's okay, that he's happy sitting with me, telling him he shouldn't feel he has to.

"No, it's fine. I like it."

One day, she says, "Do you mind sitting with Stephen, if I just pop to the corner shop? I'll only be a couple of minutes…"

She hates asking for help. I wonder why Jamie's different.

Another day, he brings a cluster of balloons, tied together with string, over the wall. It makes for a clumsy entrance, but he lands on his feet, balloons in hand.

He cuts one of the balloons loose, and stands in front of me with it, smiling as though it's the best thing ever. He throws it towards my head, it bounces off my nose and he catches it. Not fair—I wasn't ready! He throws again; my head jerks randomly which punches it back to him.

I did that! Did you see it?

"Awesome, mate!" Jamie cheers. "Ready for another one?" And he throws it again.

My hand spasms and connects with the squeaky yellow rubber, trapping it in my lap. I try to pat it back to him, and eventually a slight movement from me and the wind together pushes it to the floor.

For the first time in several years, I'm playing a game. My head doesn't move next time—it just boings off my forehead as it would any inanimate object—and I make a frustrated clicking noise. Jamie tries some keepie-uppies with it, but the wind blows it away and he chases after it, tripping over Mum's raised flowerbed. I laugh—my gurgling, gargling laugh.

We play for a while longer. I concentrate really hard and my head occasionally moves at just the right moment.

I picture myself running around the garden in football-style knee-sliding celebration. I was a good footballer, at school—the top goal scorer for two seasons running. I stopped playing when I started uni—I always thought I'd go back and find a small-town team to join, but I never had time. I've got lots of time now.

The spasms grow more frequent, no longer controllable.

"You're getting tired."

I yawn and grin. I'm tired in a totally new way.

Jamie puts the balloon in my lap and finishes the coffee Mum left on the table for him earlier.

"See you later, Steve." He waves and leaps back over the wall. I really wish I could do that.

***

My back garden is an ocean, filling with relentless, torrential rain. I sit in my room, watching the rain splatting against my window. At first, I try to look through the rivulets, to the garden beyond, to the patio where I spend so much of my time. But after a while, I simply watch the water, drip after drip chasing down the pane.

If the rain continues, it'll flood the yard, the water level will rise high enough to shake the house from its foundations. We'll sail on our newly formed ocean, alongside all the other houses on the street. We'll be a massive flotilla of unconventional boats, searching for a new land.

I close my eyes to listen as the storm escalates. It's an ominous and disturbing noise. It's the setting for a horror film—a dark and stormy night, while murderers stalk outside, or vampires and poltergeists bang on the front door to be let in.

Or it's the soundtrack of a romantic walk in the park. Two lovers kissing while rainwater drips down their faces, hurrying home to strip off and dry themselves beneath a warm duvet.

Or it could even be the drone of a saturated camping trip—rain tapping onto canvas and seeping through weathered seams. Outside the fire previously built to cook beans and sausages has been doused and wild animals are circling.

I can't remember if it's a dream or a memory. We used to camp a lot when I was young, when Dad was still around, and I'd run to the river and swim while he set up the tent.

The house is boring; the walls are creeping towards me. Mum passes in and out of my room, bringing drinks and holding the straw to my mouth, or carrying laundry and refilling my drawers with t-shirts and underwear. I hear the snarl of the dying vacuum cleaner and the washing machine's final ear-piercing spin and the phone ringing. It's louder inside than out.

I miss the birds and the purring traffic, the wind in the trees and the reverberation of those helicopters.

I watch the rain falling from the blackened sky, puddles forming on the lawn where the ground isn't fully flat, a cat sheltering under the patio table, poised like an elegant porcelain ornament.

Mum wheels me to the kitchen for lunch. She bustles around, chatting breezily, or singing along to CDs—artists I'm surprised my mother is even aware of, like Slipknot and Fozzy. She has a soft melodic voice, it's bizarre to hear her singing heavy metal.

"I had that dream again," she says, "the one where I'm playing piano. I was on a stage, dressed up in full concert-style regalia." She laughs, then smiles poignantly. "It was a beautiful burgundy taffeta dress. I looked so…" She languishes for a moment, and when she returns, her voice is crisp and practical. "Right, let's eat. Omelette or baked beans?"

She had lessons when she was younger. Her mother—my grandmother—thought it essential although Mum showed no aptitude. Month after month she was forced to sit in a draughty church hall in front of an instrument which became an adversary.

When I dream, it's of walking. Just that. Marching along a busy main road, on my way to work, or wandering around a supermarket picking up a few things for dinner. I guess we all dream of the things we can't do in real life.

Jamie told me he dreams of skydiving even though he's afraid of heights.

***

Tonight, my back garden is a spaceship, and we're flying into the dark, limitless universe. Behind us, below us, the Earth is vanishing, smaller and smaller until it's just a pinprick, the way Venus or Mars looks to us normally. I am weightless, unrestrained, wild.

Or, rather, Jamie has carried me from my chair and laid me on a blanket, with another wrapped around my shoulders so I'm snuggled up and cosy. My head rests on a pillow, shared with Jamie. My body is stiff and unyielding, awkwardly moulded on the hard ground.

Earlier, we watched the sun set behind the terrace of houses that backs onto ours. We listened to the evening birdsong and chirping insects. It chilled and the sky turned violet then indigo. It's almost black now—stars sparkle as if sequins have been sewn onto velvet. Jamie points out some of the constellations, Orion and The Plough.

"And that's..." He laughs and lowers his hand. "Oh, okay, I'm out. That's all I know."

He falls silent, but I like it that way. For a moment, between my wheezing breaths, I'm in the void of space, lost in the vastness. The closest, brightest stars flicker blue or red—actually twinkling like in the nursery rhyme. The more I stare at them, the more prominent they seem. The Milky Way, at first a faint blur, emerges like grains of sand, more expansive and distinct as my eyes grow accustomed. Wherever I look, more and more stars appear.

The International Space Station passes by, masquerading as a shooting star or an alien visitor who's decided against landing on our primitive planet.

Oh, to fly above the world, to gaze upon billions of people, to watch dawn break and dusk fall in the blink of an eye. To dive into the pool of space, to swim past planets and suns, through infinite-coloured galaxies, patterns spinning and evolving like a kaleidoscope.

I zoom towards them, lifting off from the ground, hurtling up and far away. Passing through our solar system, past Jupiter and Saturn, past Neptune and cruising into outer space. Stars become larger and more yellow, like our sun—the heat burns my skin as I soar past them—and I'm immersed in the beauty of it all.

I'm an explorer, a traveller, a fighter in a space war. The air is pure and frozen out here. I plunge onward, my legs kicking and my torso twisting. I don't want to go back to Earth, to my garden, to my chair.

Jamie coughs or sneezes or snores, and I am me again. Tiny, on a tiny planet, and the night sky is enormous and overwhelming.

***

My back garden is crowded, full of chatter and music and laughter. I am thirty.

I have a badge and a party hat and balloons tied to my chair. I have cards and guests—I didn't realise I knew so many people.

Jamie takes photos and videos. He stands in front of me and I force my brightest smile which makes my cheeks hurt a little. People bend over so their heads are level with mine, or crouch down so they're looking up to me, arms draped around my shoulders, posing for the next shot. Jamie scrolls through the photos, showing them to Mum, and then to me.

I haven't seen myself for a very long time. I don't look how I remember. I'm a stranger. My face is gaunt, my hair is shorter than before, my eyes are red and dry and unfocussed. My mouth, unless I concentrate really hard, is slack with a gawky pout.

My hand reaches towards the picture Mum's holding and tries to push it away. I'm not me anymore, and I don't want the reminder. I'm not the guy who cycled to university and partied at the weekends and took a different girl home every month.

These people in my garden are not my friends—they're Mum's and possibly Jamie's too. Not mine. I don't have any; how could I?

When I had my accident, I'd left home several years before. Mum had a new relationship and was planning a holiday of a lifetime to New Zealand. I visited for Sunday lunch every couple of weeks and listened to her unsubtle hints about marriage and grandchildren. One day, I'd say with a soft smile.

She didn't hesitate when I was released from hospital—didn't suggest a care home or carer. She converted her dining room into a bedroom and took a sabbatical from work.

She thought I would die, that sitting beside my bed would be the last memory she'd have of me—I heard her talking to Jamie about it, once. She's pouring herself a glass of wine now, looking melancholy behind a happy facade, like she wishes everyone was gone and she was sitting here alone.

***

My back garden has reverted to a prison. I wait for Jamie, but he doesn't come. I check the time constantly—when my chair faces south-west, there's a large ornate clock hanging on the wall in front of me. I bought it for Mum, when everything was different. The garden was her sanctuary before it was mine—hers was filled with dinner parties and music and laughter.

She's tired now. Her face only smiles when she looks at me, her proper smile. She bustles out to bring my lunch. She sits beside me to feed me the blended mush. From another garden, the smell of barbecue makes my mouth water. I pretend I'm eating steak, that I'm biting into a thick succulent burger.

Time ticks on, one laborious second at a time. I don't know how long I've known Jamie; my memory sucks. It could be two weeks, or two years. Equally, I don't know how long I've been waiting for him to come back—a day, a week, longer, less? He could have just popped home to put the oven on. He might be on a world cruise.

The walls that have been expanding are contracting again, pushing closer, until—even with a clear blue sky above me, and the sound of birds and traffic and the life beyond—I'm trapped.

***

My back garden is a faraway land, filled with giants and dragons and warriors. Jamie makes it so.

He comes through the front door this afternoon, carrying a large cumbersome box. He sets it on the patio with a groan.

"This is my new book," Jamie explains, taking several copies from the box, The Last Dragon by James Munro.

The cover has gold lettering and an illustration of a knight sitting beside a dragon. They seem to be huddling together, as if sheltering from the cold or sharing a secret.

"I thought you might like to hear me read some of it to you?" He stops abruptly and shakes his head. He drops the books back into the box. "Sorry. Silly idea. You probably wouldn't be interested. It's a children's book…"

Yes, yes I would. An author! I know a real-life author, how cool is that.

"Yes, he would," Mum says, bringing out a pot of coffee and two mugs on a tray at just the right time. "See, he's staring straight at you—that's a yes." She ruffles my hair and kisses my cheek. "Is it okay if I join you? I'd love to hear it too. Congratulations, by the way."

She pours the coffee and Jamie holds up the book; he reads the title and his name as if he's a children's television presenter. He folds back the cover and clears his throat. I like listening to him— it's different from when he's just talking normally to me. His voice is excited and calm, calamitous and curious, soft and harsh, bright and loaded.

The hero is called Stephen, like me. He named his character after me. He catches my eye when he says the name for the first time and smiles. I'm transported to the rocky terrain of his fictional world, to the mountain that houses ogres and rises high into the clouds. I'm attacked by dragons and saved by a band of friends who work together to defeat the repulsive giants.

We're still outside when the sun sets. Jamie's girlfriend Rachel is here too, and they've ordered a takeaway. Mum lights several candles and wraps my blanket around my shoulders.

***

My back garden is a doorway. Jamie has his hands on the handles of my wheelchair, and Mum's fussing behind him.

"You know what to do if…? He might choke when… He gets anxious in…" There are a thousand thoughts running through her head and she can't keep track of them all. She opens the bag to double-check the contents. She takes my hat off and puts it back on again. She lists all the things that might go wrong, but probably won't.

"You can come with us, if you want to," Jamie says, but he doesn't mean it.

When he first suggested taking me out, he said it was going to be a lad's day, he said it would be nice for Mum to spend some time having fun. So, she's going for a glass of wine with Rachel and have her nails done, and we're going to the park for a picnic. We'll sit by the lake and watch the ducks. Jamie's tied a balloon to my chair, too —I catch sight of it in my peripheral vision as it bobs on the breeze.

"We'll be a couple of hours at the most," Jamie adds. "We'll be back before you are."

Mum stands back and claps her hands together. "I know. You're right." She's probably frowning. I can't see her because she's still behind me, but she frowns and over-thinks a lot, so it's a natural assumption. "It's always me, you see, taking care of him. I'm not sure what to do without…"

She sweeps down and kisses my cheek. "Have a nice time." She kisses Jamie's cheek too. "Thank you." And leaves quickly.

It's just me and Jamie now, in the back garden. He stands behind me and grabs the handles, pushing me back and forth, testing out the motion, the effort he needs to apply. He opens the gate and we both stare into the abyss of the back lane. He wheels me forward and we draw level with the exit. I feel like I'm standing at the door of a plane, fifteen thousand feet in the air, waiting to jump. It's scary and exhilarating, but I'm glad I'm doing it with a friend.

STORY CREDITS

The Clock in My Mother's House Runs Backwards appeared on the Fairlight Books website (2020)

The Woman in the Van longlisted in the Commonwealth Short Story Prize (2018)

Vera Says... appeared on the Flash Fiction Magazine website (2018)

All the Magpies Come Out to Play appeared on the Fairlight Books website (2021)

A Thousand Pieces of You shortlisted in the Elbow Room short story competition (2016) and longlisted in the CAS Short Story Competition (2022)

Click longlisted in both Bath Short Story Award and Colm Tobin Short Story Award (2018), and appeared on the Fictive Dream website (2019)

One Minute Silence was a finalist in the Globe Soup Short Story Competition (2021) and notable contender in the Bristol Short Story Prize (2020)

Black Dog longlisted in the Reflex Fiction competition and appeared in their anthology of winners (2019, 2020)

The Fear of Ghosts won first place in the Dark Tales Story Competition and appeared in their anthology of winners (2017, 2019)

Adventures in My Own Back Garden appeared in the When Words Fail, Music Speaks anthology (2017)

ACKNOWLEDGEMENTS

This collection has been compiled with thanks to the editors and judges who published and commended these stories over the past few years.

Huge thanks to J.S. Watts, Anne Goodwin, Kyra Lennon, and Jemma Crawford for their help at various stages of this process.

Also to my husband Peter, and to Artoo my canine muse. And to Kimberley, Luisa, Shelagh, and Helen for supplying coffee, cake, and good company.

ABOUT THE AUTHOR

Annalisa Crawford lives in Cornwall, UK, with a good supply of moorland and beaches to keep her inspired. She lives with her husband, two sons, and dog.

Annalisa writes dark contemporary, character-driven stories, with a hint of the paranormal.

She is the author of four short story collections, and her novels Grace & Serenity (July 2020) and Small Forgotten Moments (August 2021) are published by Vine Leaves Press.

For more information visit
www.annalisacrawford.com

Printed in Great Britain
by Amazon

29152362R00065